A Crazy Ghetto Love Story

A Crazy Ghetto Love Story
-A Novel Written By-
Linette King
Copyright © 2015 by True Glory Publications
Published by True Glory Publications
Join our Mailing list by texting TrueGlory to 95577

Facebook: Author Linette King

Cover Design: Michael Horne
Editor: Artessa La'Shan Michelé

Acknowledgements

First I have to give thanks to God! Without him, I am nothing. I have been through so much this year alone but with God, my family and friends, I've been able to climb each mountain of pain. A lot of people wonder how I do it but I don't know; I only know why I do it. Everything I do is for my children: Aaliyah, Alannah and Jaye.

To my supporters: You guys are freaking awesome! Thank you!

To my readers: Thanks for reading! I hope you enjoy this just as much as you enjoyed Addicted to him if not more!

I lost my daddy while writing this book. Thinking about all of the crazy things he use to say has helped me push through it! He once told my oldest sister that he's so tough he can chew a quarter up and spit out nickels! He told my cousin he's been reincarnated twice already. In 1936 he was bull, in 1953 he was a cockroach and now he's him! He told another cousin that he can jump so high that one day he was playing basketball and during the first quarter he went up for a rebound and when he came back down it was the third quarter! He told another cousin that he runs so fast that when he was playing baseball he hit the ball going straight for the pitcher. Well the pitcher ducked and when he made it to second base the ball hit him and he tagged himself out! We have so many awesome funny stories involving him! To my family: he lives on through us!

Rest in peace daddy. Charles Raynard Robertson 3/25/61 - 11/23/15

King Kong still got nothing on you!

Life's short so love freely, forgive quickly and live joyously!

This book is a complete work of fiction. If a name or situation sounds familiar it is completely coincidental.

Enjoy!

Prologue

Vanessa Broughton and her older brother Wayne were as thick as thieves growing up. They did everything together, being that they were just four years apart. Wayne was the oldest but Vanessa was the leader. Together, they would cause mischief and mayhem throughout the neighborhood. See, they both knew right from wrong and Wayne never wanted to do anything but Vanessa had a way of changing his mind. She had him wrapped around her pinky finger, in a way only a baby sister could.

The only person who could control Vanessa was her mother Karen. Sadly, she died from breast cancer when Vanessa was only eight years old. After the death of her mother, there was nothing anyone could say or do to stop her from doing exactly what she wanted to do.

Michael, the kids' father and a policeman, was so heartbroken over his wife's death that he pretty much let the two of them get away with murder, literally.

Across town, Chris Butler had no life of luxury. Not knowing who neither his father nor mother was left Chris in a cold world alone, going from foster home to foster home.

He ran away from each home until he was thirteen years old. This is when he linked up with James, Frankie, Steve and Phatty G. They lived in a CO-ED group home until Steve turned eighteen and was able to get an apartment in his name.

Together, they robbed drug dealers who didn't live near them to survive. Chris, being the youngest, was often caught by the police and sent back to another home, where he would eventually escape from.

Chris didn't trust anyone but his brothers and sister, Frankie. Although none of them were actually related, blood couldn't make them any closer. They would each take a bullet and die for the other.

Vanessa Broughton

Every day, I wake up missing my mom. She was my all-time favorite person. The only person that I never smart mouthed! The only person that understood these urges I've been having for as long as I can remember. Now she's gone and ever since then, I've been wreaking havoc on these bitches!

I tried doing the good thing because after she died, my dad told me she would want me to be the good girl I was to her for everyone. That lasted about a month because being good was boring as fuck! Not to mention, not having her to talk my urges down weren't helping me either!

Time waits for no one, so why the fuck am I thinking before I act or speak? Hell, do you know what I could have done in the time it took me to think about something I'm going to say or do any fucking way?

That following month, I was beyond over the condolences and people telling me everything was going to get better! I remember I was sitting outside on the front lawn when Ms. Jackson came outside with her mom, and they were sitting on their porch next door. Anyway, I'm playing, minding my own damn business when Ms. Jackson calls me over. "C'mere Nessa, Sweetie," she called me. I tried ignoring her but she kept calling me. I walked up to her porch but I didn't say anything I just looked at her. "How are you?" she asked, pissing me off. I mean, why everybody wanted to keep talking about the shit?

I never understood how me telling a person how I felt was going to help my situation. It doesn't matter what I say because at the end of the day, my mom will still be dead! I didn't feel like answering her, so I just turned to walk away. "The pain will fade away with time baby!" she yelled after me, stopping me dead in my tracks.

Before I knew it, I had done ran up the porch and pushed Ms. Jackson off of it! "Have you lost yo mama? No, the bitch sitting right here, so don't tell me how long it takes!" I yelled, looking down at her before hopping off the porch and going back home.

Later on that day, my dad attempted to talk to me but I didn't respond to a thing he said. His parenting sucked and he never told me to remove my headset, knowing damn well I couldn't hear a thing he was saying. That was the last time he ever tried to fuss with me.

Now, Wayne's ass was a different story! He stayed down my throat getting on my fucking nerves. When I turned ten, my dad bought me a b.b. gun and I shot Ms. Jackson's poodle in the head, and Wayne made me go apologize.

I was so pissed off because she wouldn't stop crying long enough for me to tell her I was sorry. I still laugh when I think about the face she made when I told her the pain will fade away with time! She launched at me too, like she wanted to fight but Wayne caught her before she could connect with me. Since she thought she wanted to fight me, I had a trick for her ass.

Later on that night, I grabbed a cup of water and poured it, along with a bottle of baby oil, all over her front and back porch. Afterwards, I went home and got in the bed. When I woke up, there was an ambulance outside taking her mom who had fallen and apparently broken her pelvic bone to the hospital. I watched from my bedroom window until she looked up at me. I smiled then winked before closing my curtain.

My dad never mentioned anything to me but Wayne asked me over 100 times if I had anything to do with it. He eventually put me on punishment and my dad let him.

They didn't take my b.b. gun from me, so I would just shoot random animals from my window. I got so good I could shoot a squirrel from five houses over! I had done shot everybody's pets and Ms. Jackson would send all the owners to our house.

My dad always had my back though because he knew I hadn't left out of the house and he didn't think I was as good of a shot as I was.

Enough about all of that, it's my birthday bitches! Today is May 28 and I just turned twenty-four. Oh yeah, I'm Vanessa Broughton, by the way! The guys my age don't really pay me any attention because truth be told, I have nothing to look at. I have a cute face, I'm light skinned, petite with long jet black hair. I'm 5'4" and I spend most of my time studying weapons and perfecting my craft.

Every so often, my best friend Alexis will get me out of the house, so we can go out and have fun. Alexis is the complete opposite of me with a shape to die for! She's dark skinned with an ass so big you can sit your drink on it, along with a small waist and breasts. She's so outgoing, fun, and energetic. Sometimes I think my mom sent her to me because the only time I don't want to kill someone is when I'm with her.

I don't get to go to her house as much as I'd like to because she has a brother that Wayne doesn't want me anywhere near. His name is Jerry and if I were to have a dream guy, it would be him. Jerry is only a year older than me. He's taller, which is a plus, and those tattoos will make any girl go crazy! Jerry has the perfect skin tone, not too dark or too light. I've had a crush on him since Alexis and I became friends! The problem is he doesn't ever look my way!

ring, ring *ring, ring* *ring, ring*

"Hello," I answered out of breath. I was flipping the covers everywhere in my bed trying to find my phone.

"Happy Birthday to you! Happy Birthday to you! Happy Birthday best friend ever! Happy Birthday to you!" Alexis sang as soon as I answered the phone.

"Thanks girl," I replied smiling.

"Ew! Go brush your teeth!" she said, laughing into the phone. I did a quick breath check and hopped out of my bed heading towards the bathroom.

"I bet she checked her breath like I can actually smell it through the phone." I heard her say to someone else before they started laughing.

"Bitch, fuck you! Who you talking to anyway?" I asked.

"My boo! We're on our way to get you, so get dressed! I have a surprise for you!" she cooed into the phone.

"Alright," I said, hanging the phone up. I wonder what they have up their sleeves. I'm not too fond of surprises but I know it's good coming from Alexis.

Alexis and Phatty G have been dating for a while now and he mellows her out. He doesn't say much around me, so it's pretty crazy that he's in on the surprise. He seems a bit too rough around the edges for Alexis but if she likes it, then I love it. She's always talking about how she fell in love with his height and eyes long before she fell in love with him. The nigga is like 6'2" with green eyes. Hell, I'd date him based off of appearance but he doesn't look at me. Nobody looks at skinny ole me! Hell, I'm still a virgin! I've never even kissed a guy!

Anyway, after I took a shower and got dressed, I noticed I had two missed calls from Alexis. I sat on my bed getting ready to call her back when she came bursting through my room door, scaring the fuck out of me! "Bitch, I could have shot you! Don't come in my room like that!" I yelled at her.

"Not from where you're sitting!" she said laughing. I slid my snub nose revolver with the pearl tip from behind my back, showing it to her. I laughed as I watched her mouth drop. "Bitch, I can't stand you, come on!" she said, walking out of the door.

Alexis is the only person, other than my mom, that I told about my urges. I pretty much tell her everything, she's my walking diary. Anyway, she knows I have different types of weapons all over the house and I've shown them to her. What she didn't understand is that there is always one within reach when I'm home. I've been looking for a belt that I could wear to slide some in that wouldn't look bulky but I haven't had much luck with that.

I walked through our quiet townhouse following Alexis out of the door, wondering where the hell Wayne and my dad were.

We walk up to Phatty G's 2012 silver Ford Taurus and I hopped in the back while Alexis sat upfront. "Happy Birthday Vee," he said plainly.

"Thanks," I replied, just as he was pulling off.

Alexis sat up front as we cruised the streets of Brooklyn. About an hour or so later, I looked up and we were in Queens. "Why are we over here?" I asked Alexis, who looked at Phatty G before smiling. She completely ignored my question as she turned the radio up.

I sat back and folded my arms across my chest because I'd rather know what's going on than being in the blind. We rode for another thirty minutes before we pulled into the parking lot of an old warehouse. Phatty G hopped out smiling and for first time since we've met, he looked friendly. His green eyes sparkled when he looked back, gesturing for us to follow him.

I glanced back and forth between the two of them as I followed behind them cautiously. As we entered the warehouse, I saw four people I didn't recognize and stopped in my tracks. Alexis, I trust with my life, but these people here that I've never met are the ones I don't trust. Alexis stopped walking once she noticed I stopped. Her smile vanished when she noticed how hesitant I was to go further into the warehouse.

"Come on girl. These are Phat's friends and I'm about to introduce you to them before we show you what we got for you," she said, grabbing my hand and leading me to the others.

"Hey y'all, this is the birthday girl that I've been telling y'all about, Nessa!" Alexis said smiling. Everyone said Happy Birthday, except for the chick who didn't really look like a chick at all. If it weren't for her long hair, it would have taken me a while to figure out she was a woman. Everything else about her screamed MAN! She was even dressed like the guys.

"This the bitch whose skills you been bragging about? She weighs 110lbs soaking wet!" the chick said, standing to her feet. Without thinking, I grabbed five throwing stars out of the strap I keep around my calf and threw each at her, one by one. I missed her on purpose lining two on either side of her face and one right above her head. When the shock wore off, she slowly turned around to look at what I had done, while the fellas laughed.

"Well…. Happy Birthday," she said with her back still to me.

"Thanks," I replied looking at Alexis, who was standing there smiling like a proud parent.

"Ok, back to the introductions. Ole girl who just made an ass out of herself is Frankie," Alexis said making everyone laugh but Frankie. "Those other fellas are Steve, James and Chris," she said, pointing as they gave me a head nod one at a time, as she called their names.

"Let the games begin!" Phatty G said, leading the way into another room in the warehouse. I almost cried when I looked at the spread that was before me on the table! I was in heaven!

"Bitch! For me???" I asked, looking at Alexis while trying to hold back my tears. She gave me a head nod with her arms open as I ran into her and gave her a hug.

"Ok, break that shit up!" Phatty G said, causing me to laugh and run back to the table.

The table had every type of weapon I could possibly think of! There were different types of throwing stars, some with four spikes, some with five, and some shaped liked spiders! There were all different types of knives with different blades! I walked by sliding my finger across each blade. I felt like a ninja looking all of these weapons!

There were Ashiko boots that were spiked and could be used to help climb walls, a chain with a hook to help throw grenades and flash bombs, and one of those sticks, ball and chain type of deals. The ball had spikes coming out all over it. Lastly, was the blow gun to blow darts at your target and the actual darts. I've never used one but thanks to Alexis, I'll be able to. On the other side of the table were guns, but I was more excited with the blades!

"Ok Nessa, this wasn't your surprise. Come on," Alexis said, pulling me away from the table.

"Well, whose weapons are those?" I asked confused.

"They're yours from me," answered Phatty G.

"Oh my gosh! Thanks Phat!" I yelled, snatching away from Alexis to hug Phat. "Sorry," I said, pulling away after noticing how uncomfortable he got.

After hearing another door open, I picked my pace up to catch up to Alexis. "SURPRISE!" Alexis screamed excitedly.

I could see a woman tied tightly down on another table. She turned her head when she heard us enter. "Ms. Jackson?" I asked out loud.

Chris Butler

I done been through so much shit in my life, it'd take me forever and a day to tell you everything. I was born in Queens and was left on the steps of a church. My fuck ass mama didn't even care enough to wrap me up before she left me. She left ya boy ass naked on cement steps! My birthday is between November 22nd and 24th, since they don't know for sure, I just say it's November 23rd. Anyway, the church she left me at didn't want me, so they took me to the hospital. The way my life has been they should have just let me freeze to death! From what I hear, I was pretty close to it any damn way.

Anyway, I spent most of my childhood bouncing from house to house. The third home I went to was the first home I ran away from. I was eight years old when my foster mom's husband came in my room! This nigga snatched the covers off me and started pulling my pants down. I don't know who the fuck he thought I was but even at eight years old, I wasn't no dummy and I wasn't no fucking punk neither! I always kept the shank I made when I was five with me. I've just been making it better over the years. So, this nigga got my pants off but not before I woke completely up! I reached under my pillow grabbing my shank and stabbed him in his left eye with all my might! I knew I would still need my shank, so I pulled it back out and this nigga's eyeball was stuck to it. I thumped it off and slid back into my pants, while he screamed like the bitch he was. When I heard my foster mom walking down the hall, I climbed out of the window and hauled ass, never looking back!

I didn't get caught by the police until I was twelve and that shit was so crazy. I was walking out of a convenient store when this old lady was getting her purse snatched. I walked up to ole boy and hit him so hard between his eyes, he passed out. I tried to leave but the store clerk realized I had done stole some shit and grabbed my wrists before I had the chance to walk away. They sent me to juvie for a year and when I was released, I went to this CO-ED group home. One thing I learned about that experience was to mind your own damned business! If I wouldn't have been trying to help that old ass lady, I wouldn't have gotten caught stealing and gone to juvie.

Oh yeah, I'm Chris Butler. I'm a twenty-four-year-old dark skinned nigga and I'm about 5'9". All of those pushups, sit ups, and pull ups I was doing while I was locked up got me right! I got addicted to the iron and started breaking into gyms every night to continue to get my weight up. Now, these hoes were choosing.

My little young black broke ass had a different bitch every week. I had to keep them hoes in rotation, since all I had to offer was dick. I didn't want any of them figuring out that they weren't the only ones. That's why I never ignored any of them! Not even if I was with one of them. Shit, I would just pretend it was my dead beat ass mama.

When I first got to the group home, I met Phatty G and he been my nigga ever since then. Frankie, James, and Steve all came after me, and we just kind of looked out for each other. We all had been through so much already and sticking together just made things better. The group home had over fifteen kids in it at the time but we were the outcasted ones. Well Frankie, James, and Steve were because Phatty G and I were fucking them hoes in the laundry room!

Brittany was the only one that thought she was slick though. Little bitch was fucking both of us and lying like it was nothing with neither one of us. She didn't talk to us at all in front of the other girls there. The only time she talked to me is when she wanted some dick and I always gave it to her thick ass.

The other kids were able to do odd jobs at the home for extra money but there were never any jobs available when we would try to make a quick buck. After a while, we started sneaking out after bedtime, breaking in houses and stealing money. Pretty soon, we were the "It Crew" but we weren't fucking with the other people there. Jobs started coming available for us but we weren't accepting any because we had our own shit going on. Other kids tried joining us but we stuck to that "No New Friends" motto religiously!

We stayed in the home until Steve turned eighteen. Right before his eighteenth birthday, we hit three houses and four cars totaling $1,000 apiece. It was the most money any of us had ever had at one time. We put it all together to get a three-bedroom apartment in Queens. We only had to pay a $250 deposit and the first month's rent, which was $720, so we still had a little over $4000 left.

We all had different skills that made us whole as a group. Steve could pick any lock, giving us access to pretty much everything. James could steal any fucking, car so we only walked if we felt like it! Frankie is double jointed and can squeeze in damn near every space imaginable! I'm the muscle, the leader and level headed one, while Phatty G is the smooth talker. This nigga can talk his way out of any situation.

Anyway, with the money we had left over, we decided to furnish the crib. After we got a queen size bed for each room and a living room suit, we only had about $400 dollars left, so it was time to scout out new targets to make more money. That's when we decided to rob drug dealers. It was Phat's idea to rob the flashy niggas, since they wanted to throw it in our faces. I remember our first big heist like it was yesterday.

Steve made a long trip to Newark to see what this cat name Easy E was working with, before we made the trip together. He used $300 of the $400 we had left to get a motel in Newark, while he scoped the scene out on Easy E. Steve don't do the scouting every time, since we normally take turns scoping someone out. This cat was just way too flashy and from what Steve called and told us, he wasn't too smart either. Steve had only been out there three days and already knew where three trap houses were. Shit, that's really all we needed and we could chill out for a while.

I told Steve to pretend to be a smoker that night to see how late people would be there at night. I couldn't believe my fucking ears when Steve called saying they close the shop at 10:30, and he was a few minutes too late.

Now, why the fuck would you tell a smoker your business hours? What type of shit is Easy running if he's letting them mufuckers close down shop? Shit, the drug game is a 24-hour business and he's slipping. I heard his murder game is so on point that the bodies are never found. That shit didn't scare me though because if he ever tried to kill me, his body would be the one missing.

So, we load up in a Camry James stole a few minutes ago. I look over at Frankie, who is rolling up like we ain't about to do a job and need her on point. "Bitch, what the fuck are you doing?" I asked with an attitude.

"Nigga what the fuck it look like I'm doing?" she asked me.

"Bitch, don't smoke that shit til after we're in, out, and on our way back home!" I yelled at her as she rolled her eyes. "I hope them bitches roll right on out yo head," I said, turning back around.

James laughed as he continued to make our drive to meet up with Steve. Phatty G, not being much for words, just shook his head. We ended up needing to stop for gas, so we pulled over so I could change the license plates. Frankie's ass was supposed to had done the shit but she was still pissy about how I talked to her earlier. I swear, bitches always want to be treated like niggas but get in their feelings when you talked to them like one.

After I was done, we stopped at a gas station and surprisingly, Phatty G wanted to get out and pay. This nigga never wants to get out and pay or pump, so I knew something was up with his ass! It wasn't until he walked out of the store with a dark skinned chick with the biggest ass I've seen in a while and small titties that I realized why he wanted to go in. They chopped it up for about ten minutes before he finally brought his ass on to the car.

"Damn nigga, that bitch got us behind schedule! Chris, you need to check ya boy while he trying to get his dick wet!" Frankie said, causing me to laugh. The way she hates on the nigga whenever he talking to a bitch got me thinking she trying to get fucked or he done already fucked her.

"Bitch, don't worry about me and my dick. That's gone be wifey there and she don't even know it yet," he replied and Frankie's face turned red. The rest of the ride was silent with everyone probably thinking about what was about to go down.

We pulled up to the motel and blew, so Steve could come on out before he gave us directions to the first trap house. We pulled up on the block shutting our lights off and parking a few houses passed the target house. Just like clockwork, them niggas started cutting lights off and locking the house up. These niggas have no type of training because they were all fucked up, laughing and talking with hoes as they hopped in one truck and drove away.

I waited five minutes before giving orders. "Steve, I want you to pick the locks. Look in the windows first to see if you see a home alarm system. James, I want you to stay put, give us ten minutes and crank the car up. Frankie, I want you to stumble to the door and knock like you need a hit, so we can be sure everyone is gone. Phat, you're with me," I said before hopping out of the car.

"Bet," everyone said in unison, before we all filed out of the car and getting into motion.

I signaled for Phat to stand on one side of the house while I stood on the other. Frankie knocked and swayed from side to side. "Yo!" I heard someone yell from the opposite end of the door.

Frankie looked at me as I motioned for her to continue. "I need it bad," she pleaded, sounding like a damn smoker for real.

"We closed baby," he said and opened the door.

"You by yaself daddy?" she asked, scratching her arms.

"Naw, my patna in there but he sleep," he answered as he looked behind him.

"I'll suck yo dick," she said as she still scratched her arms. That's all she had to say to get her in the house.

I looked through the window and I could see him leading her out of the living room. "Fuck," I said under my breath. I walked up to the front door and tried my luck. "Bingo!" I said out loud. This dummy done left the damned door unlocked. I turned around, waving Phat in behind me. When I turned the corner, Frankie had ole boy hogtied with her foot on his back. I'm not gone lie that shit had my dick so hard! "Where his friend?" I asked Frankie.

"He lied. He's here alone," she answered me. I heard movement behind me causing me to jerk around with my .45 drawn but it was Steve. This nigga had done already raided the place.

"You bitches don't know who you fucking with!" the guy said right before Frankie stomped his head, causing it to hit the floor. I watched as his eyes rolled and he shook his head trying to focus.

"Are you gonna tell us?" I asked with a smirk.

"I'm gone kill all you niggas!" he said as he spat blood out of his mouth. "And you bitch-" he paused, glancing up at Frankie. "I'm gone fuck you real good, make you suck my dick, then kill you real slow," he continued and smiled up at her. She removed her silencer, attaching it to the gun before shooting him in his head.

"Let's go," I said to everyone as we headed out of the front door. We hopped in our car and headed to the next trap house. It was well past closing time but people were still hanging around. I guess only that one had a closing time. We watched them from our cramped up positions in the car.

"Man Steve, I thought you said they close at 10:30. I got shit to do," Phatty G said to Steve.

"I know you ain't rushing for no bitch!" Frankie said to Phatty G.

"Bitch, didn't I tell you to stop worrying about my dick? Do you want some? You want me to fuck you?" he asked Frankie, putting her on the spot. She started looking at all of us with her face turning red.

"Chill out Phat," I said to him.

"Naw man, fuck that! Bitch always got some shit to say about what I'm doing like I'm fucking her. She don't do that shit to y'all bruh!" he said, pissed off. I glanced at the house because they were starting to make too much commotion.

After noticing that they weren't paying attention to their surroundings, I turned back around in my seat. "Listen Frankie, Phat ain't yo dude so whatever he has going on ain't got shit to do with you," I said calmly to Frankie and she rolled her eyes.

"I hope them bitches get stuck like that!" Phatty G said, which caused me to sigh heavily.

"Phat man, chill the fuck out sometimes, damn! Whatever you trying to do will still be there when we get back," I said to Phatty G. At this point, my patience was thin as fuck and I really wanted to just hop out of the car blasting. I glanced back and noticed that there were only three guys left standing outside joking.

I could tell Frankie still had an attitude but I didn't understand her problem. James and Steve were both just chilling and Phatty G was texting. "I need everybody's head in the game because it's looking like this take down ain't gone be as easy as the other one," I said and waited on a response from someone but got nothing. I could tell Frankie relaxed a little bit and Phatty G put his phone away, so we were heading in the right direction.

About ten minutes later, the three guys that were outside all went inside the house, which would make taking it down harder. I couldn't send Frankie up to the door because they may not fall for it. I'm sure all three dudes wouldn't agree to having a random crackhead they don't know come in to suck their dicks.

I rotated a bit in my seat and watched the house. I saw a light upstairs shut off that I hadn't realized was on, so it could be more than three guys inside the house. "Frankie, I want you crouched behind the bushes next to the door. Still got the silencer attached?" I asked her.

"Yes," she answered.

"Ok, shoot anyone that comes out the front door that isn't one of us," I said to her. She rolled her eyes and nodded her head. We're going to have to sit down and talk about this attitude she got later because now it's time for business. "Steve, I want you to pick the lock of the back door and the rest of us will be back there with you. We're going in laying everybody out that's breathing and taking all of their money. We don't sell or do drugs, so leave 'em there," I said as everyone nodded their heads.

I hopped out of the car and watched as everyone followed suit. Frankie and Chris crept to the front of the house while we headed to the back. Out of nowhere, I heard a dog growling and if I ain't scared of shit else, I'm scared of dogs! I turned just in time to see a Pitbull leaping off of a table dead at me. I just stood there frozen, watching the dog in midair before I'm pushed hard to the grown. I looked up and Phatty G had his knife out, stabbing the Pitbull in his neck and causing the dog to yelp out in pain. I looked up at the window and noticed a light come on and the blinds shift. I rolled closer to the house and Phatty G balled up under the dog while simultaneously breaking his neck. A few minutes later, the light shut off and we all stood still waiting for someone to come out and check things out.

We made our way to the back door and stood back keeping watch, while Steve picked the lock. He's getting better and better at it because this time it took him less than thirty seconds, and we were in a laundry room. "Man, I gotta dip on outta here in a few." I heard one voice say.

"Why man? You know E wants someone here round the clock," another voice said.

"Man, he ain't paying us enough to miss out on everything being here all night," the first voice responded.

"Shit, bring them hoes here like Monte. Shit, that nigga got two of 'em upstairs with him now," the second voice said. I made my way out of the laundry room slowly with Phat on my tail.

I got my machine gun style automatic pistol with a silencer attached to it and Phat had his knife. I swear Phat's an old bob the builder ass nigga! He hated guns but he would kill you with a knife or anything else he can get his hands on. The man beat one of his foster parents with a hammer before!

I stayed close to the wall as I looked both ways before I entered the kitchen. I could still hear the guys talking as I made my way into the living room where they were.

I heard coughing and when I looked back, James' ass was choking, probably on his own damn spit. "What the fuck is that?" I heard a voice say. I hurried around the corner, sending three bullets into the chest of one of the guys with one squeeze of the trigger. I was about to shoot the other one but Phat had done leaped over the couch and grabbed him in a sleeper hold and lying him on the ground. I was about to tell him we couldn't leave anyone alive but he took his knife and slid it across his throat from ear to ear.

I looked back at James, who had fixed himself some juice, and shook my head then headed up the stairs. I opened three doors before I got to the one the guy they called Monte and two bitches were in. I couldn't believe my eyes but Monte was tied up on the bed and his mouth was gagged. The bitches were butt ass naked with one laying on the floor, while the other one was trying to suck the life out of her pussy! These thick bitches were going at it and I could feel my dick rising to the occasion. I tried shaking the shit off but the bitch on the floor started nutting and moaning, and all I could hear were moans and slurping. Right when I was about to walk in the room, the one that was on the bottom did some kind of move with her leg making them switch positions. She started sucking one nipple while pinching the other one before switching. The other bitch was moaning like crazy. My dick was so hard the shit was starting to hurt and it pressing against my zipper. I was going to let the bitches finish first but I needed to get back home and hop in some pussy now.

I walked completely in and sent three bullets into the chick on top and watched as she dropped dead on top of the other chick. She laid on the ground screaming until I silenced her with three bullets to the head, which caused it to explode. Her brain matter was everywhere! I looked at the guy on the bed, who had his eyes closed pretending to be asleep, not knowing that wouldn't help him. I emptied the clip in him for trying to play me.

When I made it back downstairs, Steve and Phat had so much shit bagged up that we wouldn't be able to go to the next trap house because we ran out of room in the trunk. When we walked outside, James was in the driver's seat, sipping on his glass of juice and Frankie was in the back smoking. I hopped in the front and Phat hopped in the back after we loaded the money up. It was a long silent drive home. The only thing I heard was Phatty G texting on his phone and Frankie sucking her teeth.

That was a few years ago and a lot has changed since then. Our group is still together physically but we're broken mentally. Everybody has their own thing going on. Steve and James aren't growing as individuals; they just do whatever we tell them to do without questioning anything. There's been a few times where James tried to go off and do some solo shit and each time, he paid a terrible price. Because of that, he's been hospitalized three times, once for a stab wound and twice for gunshot wound! Phatty G is in love with the chick he met that day at the gas station. I think her name is Alexis, I can't be sure because he doesn't really bring her around much. Frankie's ass hates her but the only reason I think she don't like her is because she likes Phat. Alexis seemed ok to me when I met her and she makes my boy happy, so she's cool in my book.

Anyway, I guess she was bugging him about her best friend's birthday and coming up with ways to surprise her. From what Phat has told me, the chick is crazy! He told me one time when she was on punishment, she shot all of her neighbor's pets with a damned bb gun. Everybody thought it was funny except Frankie. Frankie is also the only one against helping Alexis with her friend's birthday surprise.

So, Alexis told us that her best friend, Vanessa, had been having a lot of problems with one neighbor in particular named Ms. Jackson. She asked Phat if we could take her from her home as part of Vanessa's surprise. I didn't agree with the shit but I'll always have Phat's back. I really didn't understand why she wanted us to take the damn lady. Frankie was the only one who didn't help with anything. We took the bitch without a hitch and tied her up on a table in an old warehouse Steve bought. Phat had done ordered the girl so many weapons online as a birthday gift that I thought they were preparing for war.

Phat wanted us to meet them at the warehouse and when she walked in, I swear it was love at first sight. I sat there staring at her slim frame, light skin, with long jet black hair. She was beautiful and so small that I could toss her little sexy ass all around my bedroom, fucking her in fifty different positions.

Alexis' happy ass introduced us and as expected, Frankie stood up talking shit. I've grown accustomed to tuning her jealous ass out, so I couldn't even begin to tell you what she said. All I know is Vanessa shut her ass up without touching her. This bitch threw some shit I have never seen before at Frankie's ass. I stared in amazement because I didn't see where she pulled them bitches from. The way they hit the wall, we all knew that if she wanted to kill Frankie right then, she would have before any of us had time to react. That did it for me because I was gone off this chick. The bitch had me feeling like a bitch because I swear she hadn't even looked at me.

We all followed behind them into the next room where Phat's gift was. This bitch was so excited about all these knives and shit that she'd begun to seem like the female version of Phat. When he told her he bought it for her, she ran to him and hugged his neck. Shit, they should've told me to pay for it since she still hadn't acknowledged me.

Next, Alexis opened the other door where we had her neighbor tied down. I watched as Vanessa's eyes began to water, once she realized who we had tied down on the table. Fuck! I knew we shouldn't have taken that woman! She's standing here crying and shit! "Thank you so much!" Vanessa yelled and jumped up and down, confusing the fuck out of me. She gave Alexis a hug and kissed her cheek. "I swear you're the best!" Vanessa said to Alexis, before she ran into the room. I stood there confused at first but then I realized, those weren't sad tears, those were tears of joy.

Vanessa Broughton

I couldn't believe my eyes as I stood in the doorway and looked at Ms. Jackson as she looked back at me. I could feel my eyes begin to water as my body was filled with joy. She looked at me with pleading eyes and I couldn't do anything but thank my best friend! Man, she outdid herself this year with this one! I don't even care about my dad and brother not being home to tell me happy birthday anymore because all I've wanted to do for as long as I can remember was to kill Ms. Jackson... slowly.

They say snitches get stitches and she snitched on me so much growing up, they don't have enough material in the world to stitch her for everything she's ever told on me about. I looked over at Alexis with complete admiration for this. See, I know she doesn't like or understand my need to kill but she put her issues to the side for me on my big day.

I walked into the room and slid my finger across the table as I circled it. I grabbed a scalpel off the side table and slid it up and down Ms. Jackson's legs. I looked at her face and watched as the tears fell, and she shook her head no. Whoever tied her down also gagged her mouth but I think she wanted to ask me something. "Hey, if she screams, how likely is it that someone will hear her and call the police?" I asked no one in particular.

"Zero in a million," Steve answered. I smiled at him and walked closer to her head. I roughly yanked the duct tape off her mouth, then remembered that I'm going to need gloves.

When I found the gloves, I also found all of the personal protective equipment they use at the hospital. "Thanks bitch!" I said to Alexis while I laughed.

"Girl, I remembered how you did that damn dog, so I knew you would need everything!" she said to me.

She's referring to the time one of my neighbors, Pamela Knight's, dog bit the fuck out of me! I walked her dog down to her house and let her know the dog bit me and the bitch snatched the dog up and said "So, sue me!" and slammed the door in my face. I was pissed off about it and vented to Alexis and she told me to do me. A few days later, her dog walked his happy go lucky ass back in my yard and this time, I was ready for him. I chopped him up, head, legs and paws, and put him in a bag and sat it on her porch.

Ms. Jackson sent her to our house once she found him and I answered the door to her yelling and carrying on talking about I killed her dog. I said, "So, sue me!" and slammed the door in her face. She called the police but without proof, no one could do anything to me.

"Why are you doing this?" I heard Ms. Jackson ask, which snapped me back to reality. She was whimpering softly as I turned all of my attention back to her.

"You don't remember all of the drama you've caused? All of the people you sent to my house because you thought I was guilty?" I asked her because she's laying here asking why, as if she's done nothing wrong.

"You were guilty! You were killing helpless animals for nothing!" she yelled at me.

"Bitch, did you see me do it? Did anyone have any proof that I did anything? You assumed I did it and even sent the police to my house to arrest me!" I said, getting pissed off. I'm a strong believer of no telling! If somebody does some shit they know they aren't supposed to be doing and they don't get caught, who the fuck are you to tell? Hell, if someone did some shit and you only have an assumption, why the fuck are you talking? See, I don't understand people like Ms. Jackson. She's the kind of person to throw a stone and hide her hands. I would see her peeking out of her window blinds, while one of the other neighbors would come knocking on the door talking about something they thought I did.

"Can I have some privacy please?" I said while I glanced up at the door. Everyone was just standing there, looking like a deer caught in headlights. Well, everyone except Phat, he was the only one that seemed cool, calm, and collected.

"No! Please don't leave me with her! Don't you know what she's going to do to me!" Ms. Jackson yelled and cried. I watched everyone walk away one at a time. Alexis winked at me before mouthing have fun. I walked over and closed the door, "HELP! PLEASE SOMEBODY HELP ME!" Ms. Jackson yelled while she cried harder.

"AAAAARRRGGGGHHHH AAAAAHHH!" I screamed in her face. "Nobody is going to help you sugar," I said and walked back to my surgical table. I hadn't realized I sat the scalpel down. I walked back to her while I sang, "I'm sorry Ms. Jackson, wooooo, I am forreal!" Man, I was cracking myself up! "I'll probably never be able to say that again in a moment as funny as this one," I told her and laughed.

"You're the devil," she said to me and rolled her eyes.

"Na, Ms. Jackson, I'm worse," I replied. I grabbed her face and strapped her head down.

"What are you gonna do to me?" she asked while tears streamed down her face.

"Kill you," I replied calmly. I grabbed her chin and extended her smile with the scalpel. I cut from the corner of her mouth on both sides all the way to her cheeks. "Better. I always hated your fake small smile. Now you have a big one!" I said and smiled at her, as blood spilled out onto the table.

Her cries were beginning to get on my nerves so I stuffed the gag back in her mouth and taped it shut. I moved back down to her legs because I've always wanted to skin a bitch, but I've never been given the chance. I started at her feet and cut only a layer of skin off the bottom of each foot. By the time I got to her calve muscle, she had done passed out cold from the pain! I walked to the door and opened it. "Hey, can I get a bucket of ice water please?" I yelled out of the door before I closed it.

I walked back over to the table to continue skinning Ms. Jackson when Chris walked in with the bucket. "Where you want it?" he asked as he walked up to me.

"On her face," I said and pointed to Ms. Jackson. He chuckled a little bit before he dumped the bucket filled with ice water on her face.

She woke up instantly screaming. "I'm sorry Ms. Jackson," he said to her then looked at me, as we both filled the room with laughter.

It was then that I began to study him. He had smooth dark skin and the prettiest teeth I've ever seen on a man. I could see his muscles bulging through his white T shirt and I began to get hot. He was taller than me too, which was another plus and his hair was cut into a fade. "You need anything else?" he asked and looked directly at me in my eyes. He had the most intense stare ever. I could feel my heart racing as we stared at each other. I didn't break the stare until I heard soft whimpers.

"Oh, shut up, ya old hag. You will be in a better place before long," I said and grabbed the scalpel and began to cut the rest of the skin off her leg. The whole process took about three hours and Chris stayed with me the whole time. The others went on about their businesses.

After I skinned Ms. Jackson, Chris chopped her up and threw her in a trash bag. We walked out back and they had three pigs out back, and he dumped her pieces over in the pen with them. "Pigs eat any and everything," Chris said to me.

"Yea, I know," I replied and helped him dump her body parts in the pig's pen.

We went back inside and cleaned everything up before burning it in a trashcan out front. He told Alexis he would take me home once we were done, so she left with Phat. I was watching the Frankie chick mug my girl and I'm hoping I don't have to beat the fuck out of her.

"So, what's up with the Frankie chick? Why she so angry?" I asked Chris.

"Hard life I guess," he answered me.

"Well, it's gone get harder if she keep mugging my girl the way she been doing today. Ain't nobody tell her to fall in love with a nigga that don't love her back," I said as Chris' jaw dropped. I didn't say anything because I don't know what I said to make his jaw drop like that.

He stared at me for a few seconds before he began to laugh. "Man, I been saying something was up with her for the longest! Shit, I thought she just wanted to fuck him. I ain't even think she done fell in love with the nigga," he said, still laughing. I just stared back at him because I didn't see a damn thing funny about falling in love with someone who loved someone else. I mean, that had to be the worse feeling in the world. Then on top of that, she has to watch him love someone else. Naw, that shit ain't funny by a long shot. Still don't mean I won't fuck her up behind my girl though.

I turned around and headed towards the car that was left for us to get home. When I looked back, he was sitting there shaking his head and still laughing. I cleared my throat to get his attention and he hopped up and did a light jog to the car. "What's yo problem?" he asked me.

"Starved," I simply answered.

"Alright. Where to, birthday girl?" he asked.

"I don't know. Surprise me," I replied. He smiled the most beautiful smile I've ever seen on a man and all I could think about was getting away from him before I ended up like Frankie.

We rode in silence for about ten minutes before the questions started. It felt like I was being interrogated the way, he was firing off question after question. Strangely, I didn't mind. I had never had a guy pay attention to me, yet here I am in the car with a chocolate god and we're talking!

"What's on your mind?" Chris asked me. I took a moment to think about whether or not I should tell him I'm digging him. I mean I know I'm cute but nobody ever paid me any attention. He could just want me to be his friend and if I tell him how I feel, that could potentially ruin it.

"Just wondering where my dad and brother are," I half lied. I was really thinking about being his girl but at the same time, they still hadn't called me.

He didn't respond, he just continued to drive. "Asshole," I mumbled to myself.

"Excuse me?" he asked and glanced at me while driving.

"Why did you ask me what was on my mind?" I asked and rotated my body, so I could face him.

"Because I wanted to know," he answered simply. Now I'm frustrated because I thought he would be easy to talk to, at least since he asked for my thoughts. I guess he was just asking just to be asking. "If someone wants to elaborate, it's on them. If not, oh well. I asked what was on your mind because of how you were looking. When you're ready to tell me more, you will," he said to me, without taking his eyes off the road.

I turned back around and didn't say anything else until we pulled into a Wendy's parking lot. "What you getting?" he asked, as he pulled his phone out. I waited for him to send his text message before I answered him.

"Jr. Bacon cheeseburger and a coke."

"I can multi task," he stated.

"Do you want a cookie?" I asked him. He didn't respond, he just turned around to order our food. When we got our orders, and parked the car so we could eat. I sat there and wondered why we didn't go inside and sit down, instead of eating in the car.

"What's on your mind?" he asked with a mouth full of food.

"Chew your damn food up!" I said and turned my lip up at him. His phone chimed and he reached for it but I beat him to it.

"Can I check the message?" I asked. He shrugged his shoulders. I opened the messages and saw that he had been texting Frankie and someone named Brittany. The incoming message was from Brittany. "Who is Brittany?" I asked because I already knew who Frankie was.

"A bitch I'm fuckin," he answered, like it was nothing. See, I'm glad I didn't tell him I was feeling him because he obviously doesn't give a shit about women. See, my dad loved my mom and cherished the ground she walked on, so I wasn't used to this kind of talk about a woman you're sleeping with.

"Wow," I said to him and shook my head.

"What? Never ask questions when you're looking for a certain answer. Well, don't ask me cause I'm a real nigga. I ain't got time to lie about shit and have to keep up with that lie," he said to me, which caused my jaw to drop. "Pick ya lip up. That's what's wrong with women now, ya ask for a nigga to keep it real and then get in ya feelings." He continued then winked at me.

I scrolled through his messages and Brittany had sent him several pussy shots and a few shots of her tits. She had the biggest blackest nipple I had ever seen in my life. "Who the message from?" he asked, after h chewed his food up.

"Brittany," I answered.

"Word? What she said?" he asked.

"She sent a picture of her pussy," I answered as he nodded his head, while still eating.

I finished long before him so once he finished, he cranked the car back up and drove off. We didn't make it three blocks before there were lights flashing behind us. "Aw fuck!" he said. "Look, I'm fina hop out and haul ass. You can follow me and run too or stay. James stole this bitch before he brought it to the warehouse," he said in one breath, like this shit was normal. One thing for certain and two things for sure, my slim ass wasn't running no damn where and neither was him. I glanced back and noticed how tinted the windows were.

"Switch seats," I said, as I unbuckled my seatbelt.

"The fuck you doing girl?" he asked, aggravated.

"Switch seats before you stop completely. C'mon on," I said, while I climbed over to the driver's seat with him. He quickly hopped over into the passenger seat and looked at me crazy. I pulled the car over and grabbed the paperwork out of the glove compartment. I scanned over the documents and put everything back, except the registration and car insurance.

"Go to sleep," I said to Chris. He looked at me crazy before he reclined his seat and turned his face towards the door.

"Good evening ma'am," the officer said, once he reached my window.

"Good evening sir. How's everything going?" I asked him.

"Fine. Did you realize you did a roll stop back there?" he asked me.

"What's that?"

"Ma'am, how old are you?"

"I made 24 years old today!" I said and smiled.

"Really? Can I see your driver's license, registration and insurance please?" he asked me.

"Sure thing. This is my dad's girlfriend's car though, but here you go," I said as I handed him everything out the window.

He took a step back before he called my information in. "Is the young man ok over there?" he asked, as he handed me my things.

"Yes sir, I just wore him out this morning. We've been window shopping all over town. He complained the whole time, so I should be the one tired!" I said and laughed hard.

The officer joined in. "I know how he feels! The misses do me the same way! Well, y'all have a good day and take it easy on him," he said and tapped the top of the car before he walked away.

"Alright, you too," I said before I drove away.

It hadn't even been two minutes before Chris let his seat up and grilled! "Man, where the hell you learn how to do that? You and Phat related?" he asked me.

"Man, I can definitely talk myself out of trouble and no, we aren't related," I simply answered. "I remember when I use to kill the dogs and cats in my neighborhood, and the police would show up!" I laughed. "Yeah, I got a lot of practice," I said, still laughing. I glanced over at Chris, who just stared out of the window. I wanted to ask him what was on his mind but I ain't as brave as he is.

Chris Butler

I swear, ya boy slick in love with Vanessa right now. I done had plenty of bitches way thicker than she is. I love thick bitches, well I love fucking thick bitches but this little slim bitch done came through and fucked my head up in a day!

First, the bitch gets happy enough to cry because we kidnapped a neighbor that had been fucking with her for years and she finally gets her payback. Then she literally fucking killed the bitch! Now, y'all probably think she crazy but I think she's amazing! How many women you know would stand up to an old bully? Most women just talk about what they're going to do but not Vanessa! She's more action than talk and that's the type of woman I need.

She asked for privacy with the lady and we all tried to give it to her, but she was taking so long and everybody was ready to go. I needed to see if she was really going to do the shit, so I waited for her to finish while everybody else dipped out. I had my boy James go and get me a car, so we'd have transportation when she finished working.

We fed the old bitch to the pigs and Vanessa didn't even flinch. Even Frankie turns her head every time but Vanessa helped me! That shit was so player! The only thing bad I noticed is she can't handle my attitude. See, I'm a real nigga and an open book, which makes being a real nigga easier. I'm not about to lie about shit because it's way easier for me to tell you the truth. If I lie, then I have to remember what lies I told and tell another and another to cover up each one.

I was second guessing Vanessa when she wanted to read my messages. I knew them bitches were explicit and I could tell she had an attitude afterwards but shit, she's the one that wanted to read them, so I didn't feel bad. Now when we got pulled over and she smoothed talked the damn police officer, I wanted to ask her little ass to marry me. She handled that shit so good man, I swear. I was lying in the passenger seat scared as fuck. I'm surprised my damn breathing wasn't labored, as scared as I was. I wanted to hop out the fucking car and haul ass but I couldn't leave her like that, after she had done gave the man her driver's license. She ain't know shit about me, so I wasn't worried about her snitching, it was just the principle of the matter. Real niggas do real shit.

I could tell she was still bugging about my text messages but as long as she didn't express it, I wouldn't address it. Simple as that. I'm 24 years old. I ain't trying to be tied down to one mufucker no way. I don't have any kids, so I ain't really got no responsibilities other than taking care of my damn self. Now, when it's time for me to settle down, then she will be added to my list of responsibilities, but I'm not ready for all of that.

It was going on four o'clock and I've been with her all damn day but I wasn't complaining. I know Brittany sent that picture of her pussy because she wants to fuck. If I can drop Vanessa off, fuck Brittany, and then pick her back up, that would be perfect but I know it ain't gone go down like that. Oh well, I guess I'll see her again but if not, oh well.

"What you do with my phone?" I asked her.

"I think I tossed it in the glove compartment when I was getting the stuff out of it," she said pointing.

I looked in, grabbed my phone, and called Phatty G. "Yo!" he answered on the second ring.

"What's good? Where y'all?" I asked him.

"Shit, we at the crib. Y'all just now getting finished?" he asked.

"Naw, we been done. We stopped by Wendy's and ate. Yo, what's all that noise?" I asked him as I pulled the phone away from my ear.

"Frankie and Lexis. Man, they been arguing since we got here getting on my fucking nerves!" he said, and sighed heavily into the phone.

"You need to put Frankie's ass in her place dog, forreal. Especially since we about to come through and Nessa already talking about fucking her up," I said, which caused Phat to laugh.

"That bitch still fucking with my friend? Which way we're going?" Vanessa asked because her nosey ass was listening to my conversation. Phat burst into laughter in my ear.

"Bruh, you've got your hands full with her alone," Phat said, still laughing.

"I ain't got shit," I said to him.

"Cut it out man. I saw how you were looking at her earlier. I know that look anywhere," he laughed.

"We'll be there in a few minutes," I said and disconnected the call.

"What's wrong with you?" she asked me.

"Phat ass talking about I got my hands full with you, like I'm wit you or some shit," I replied and regretted it as soon as the shit left my lips. Normally, what comes out of my mouth comes out unfiltered and you can take it how you want to because I wouldn't give a fuck. The way her facial expression changed and she turned back to watch road made me question why I said it the way I said it.

"Make this next right and then a left, and we will be there," I said to her. She didn't respond, she just kept going straight. When she hopped on the bridge, I had a feeling this wasn't going to end well. "Where you going?" I asked her.

"Home," she stated simply.

"You don't wanna hang out with Lexis?" I asked her because I knew I fucked up.

"She knows where I live. If she wants to hang out, she can come there," she said and I didn't respond. I just shook my head.

She was speeding so we made it there in record time and she hopped out of the car. I hopped out and walked around to the driver's side and drove off. I guess she can't be my girl if she going to be in her feelings like that. I ain't say shit that bad to make her want to go home. I figured she just wouldn't talk to me once we got there but this bitch didn't want to be around me at all. Fuck it though.

I drove back to Brooklyn and scooped Brittany up on my way to the condo. "No call, just a show up huh?" she asked and hopped in the car.

"You want me to turn around and take you back?" I asked her.

"Naw, just talking shit. Where are we heading?" she asked.

"To the crib," I answered. The rest of the ride was silent.

I parked and we got out and made our way to the door. Phat opened it and stepped completely outside before he pulled me to the side. "Hey to you too, Phat," Brittany said as she walked around him into the house.

He gave her a head nod before he turned his attention back to me. "Yo man, what the fuck have you done?" he asked me looking serious.

"Man, it wasn't shit. Man, you know how my mouth is," I replied because it wasn't shit serious enough for him to be acting the way he acting.

"She called Lexis snapping about you being an asshole and why she went home. Got Lexis in there snapping on my ass! If I'on get no pussy tonight because of yo mouth, we gone have some problems!" he said before he turned around and walked back in the house.

I couldn't possibly give a fuck if he got some pussy or not because at the end of the day, I was about to tear into some ass right now! Fuck the dumb shit because bitches too damn sensitive these days. Sorry, not sorry! I'm just fresh out of fucks to give.

"C'mon Brit," I said and broke the stare off everybody seemed to be having with someone else. Frankie was mugging the fuck out of Alexis. Alexis was mugging Brittany. Brittany was mugging Phatty G and his ass was mugging me. Ain't shit this serious.

I walked into my room, took my clothes off, and headed to the couch in my room. "Why are you going way over there?" Brittany asked while she took her clothes off.

"Shit, we ain't fucking in my damn bed girl!" I said to her.

"We fuck in mine!" she yelled at me.

"That's yo shit! I'on fuck in my bed. I'm fuckin you on this couch, just like every fuckin body else," I said before I sat down. She stopped and folded her arms across her chest. "Look, I ain't got time for all these emotions man, is we fuckin or nah?" I asked her.

"Nah," she said as she grabbed her clothes off the floor. Fuck it.

I grabbed the remote and turned the TV on. "What are you doing?" Brittany asked me.

"The fuck it look like I'm doing?" I asked her, clearly annoyed. I just asked the bitch a second ago if we were fucking and she said no. The fuck she wants me to do, rape her? Fucking no! It's too many bitches freely fucking to chase one piece of pussy.

"What are you gonna do when I leave?" she asked me.

"Cry," I said sarcastically as I looked dead at her.

"That's what you get for not respecting me!" she said and rolled her neck.

"Bitch, you don't respect yo damn self. Clearly you missed the sarcasm but to answer your question, do you see this hard dick over here?" I asked her and pointed at my shit. She nodded her head. "I'm going to call another bitch over to make my boy go down," I continued.

"What about me?" she asked.

"Bitch, you just said you ain't want to fuck!" I said to her.

She got down on her hands and knees and crawled slowly to me. I sat back on the couch and watched TV until she made it to me. She started sucking on my dick nice and slow, deep throating my whole dick every time. Right when I was getting into it, she stopped and started jacking it with my balls in her mouth. She started humming and stroking my shit. I grabbed her head and guided her mouth back to my dick and fucked her mouth roughly until I came. She took it like a champ.

I walked over to the nightstand grabbed a condom and slid it on, on my way back to her. She already had her face down and ass up, just the way I liked it. I slid in her slowly because her pussy always gripped a nigga's dick perfectly! As much as she fucks, her shit always tight because of some pussy tightening cream her ass be using. Brittany could take dick like no other and I had ten inches to give her ass too! I was fucking her hard as fuck for talking back to me but she was creaming on my dick, making her shit wetter for me. Trying to punish her, I ended up punishing my damn self! I came a few minutes later.

Walking into the hallway ass naked was always the funniest thing to do. I don't ever have clean towels in my room, so I have to walk out and get one every time I fuck. I heard a loud gasp and when I turned around, Frankie stared at my dick with her hand over her mouth. I faced her and made my dick bounce before I turned around to get the towel. When I turned back around, she was still standing there looking stupid. I walked up to her and closed her mouth before I headed in my room.

I soaped my towel up and washed my dick and balls off before I tossed it in my dirty clothes hamper. Brittany bypassed me going into the bathroom, grabbed the towel out of the hamper before she wiped her pussy off and threw it back in there. I stood there and stared at her nasty ass in disbelief. She brushed passed me with an attitude and started getting dressed.

She kept mumbling under her breath as she got dressed. I have no idea what her problem was but she needed to calm down before she needed a ride home. She snapped her bra together and grabbed her panties, putting them on aggressively and losing her balance and falling backwards on the floor. I laughed so hard my damn stomach started hurting. When I calmed down, she was crying silently while she got dressed. "You ready to take me home?" she asked.

I walked out of the room with just my underwear on and looked for Frankie. She was in the living room watching TV alone when I found her. "Hey, can you do me a favor?" I asked her.

"I'm not taking that bitch home," she said without looking up.

"Well, is Lexis still here?" I asked her.

"Yeah but you know she ain't taking that bitch home neither," she stated. She was more than likely right, since she was mugging her when I first came in. I walked back in my room and threw my clothes on when I had a great idea.

"Hey, I need a cab. 4402 Robinhood Avenue in Brooklyn. Alright bet," I said over the phone. Why would I drive a stolen car a few blocks over when she can chill here until a cab comes to get her?

"You called me a cab?" she asked.

"Yeah. Stay in here and wait for them," I said and tossed her $100 and headed back to my room to take a shower. All I wanted was to shower and sleep.

Vanessa Broughton

I can't believe how big of an asshole Chris is! I mean seriously, who talks like that all the time? The only time it's acceptable to talk that way is when you're a child or old as fuck! Definitely not when you're our age! I don't know exactly how old he is but I know we are around the same age. He thinks talking like that without considering other people's feelings makes him a real nigga! I think not, so he needs to think again!

I couldn't wait to get my ass home so I could call Alexis and tell her about this nigga! Then he didn't even try to apologize or anything! He had to know the shit hurt my feelings for a fucking reason! Ugh! Fucking asshole!

I walked in the house and there were birthday balloons everywhere, all in my fucking way. I walked through them, popping every one within reach as I walked through. My dad was sleep in the living room but woke up when he heard all of the commotion. "Happy Birthday baby girl," my dad said as he rubbed the sleep out of his eyes.

"Thanks," I replied and walked to my room. Wayne walked out of the bathroom singing the birthday song. "Thanks," I said, cutting the song off. I walked in my room, slammed my door, and locked it.

Grabbing my phone, I called Alexis. "What's up? How far away are y'all?" she asked as she answered her phone.

"I'm home," I replied.

"What? Why?" she asked.

"Because Chris is a fucking asshole! Him and Phat were on the phone and Phat said I was a hand full and when they got off the phone, he had an attitude. So, I'm like what's up, ya know, trying to figure out what the problem is. Turns out he didn't like the way Phat worded the shit, like we together! The fuck is wrong with him? That's why I stay at home by myself because of inconsiderate assholes like him," I answered in one breath.

"I can't believe he took Phat that serious! Then, to tell you like that, like you have no feelings is preposterous!" she exclaimed. I could hear Phat in the background asking what was going on.

Knock, knock

"I gotta go Lexis," I said and disconnected the call. I hopped out of my bed to open my door. It was Wayne with a gift basket.

"Here you go, sis. It's from me and dad," he said as he handed me the basket and walked further into my room.

"Thanks," I said and sat down on my bed to open it.

The basket was huge and when I opened it, seemed like everything got bigger. There was an Amber Romance set with lotion, body spray, and body wash in it, a full Mac Makeup kit, a tennis bracelet with one stone with a gold K inside, and keys. I knew I was crying because I could feel the warm tears sliding down my cheeks. The K in the diamond is for Karen, my mom that died when I was eight years old. Wayne picked it up, so he could put it around my wrist. "I am never taking this off. It's perfect," I said to Wayne who smiled in return and handed me the keys. When I looked closer, they were keys to an Impala. I looked up at Wayne curiously. I didn't want to jump to conclusions.

"You didn't see it outside when you got here?" he asked.

"Um... noooo! Let's go!" I yelled and grabbed his arm and pulled him outside with me.

When we got outside, I saw it almost immediately! I have no idea how I missed this big ass red bow. It was a 2006 silver Impala. I walked around it and the license plate said lov3kb, and I started crying again. I looked at Wayne and his eyes were glossed over as well. I gave him the biggest hug ever and ran in the house to give my dad a hug too. I didn't even care about the asshole anymore.

"Are you ok?" Alexis said as she answered her phone.

"I'm better than ok! Bitch, I got a car!" I said excitedly.

"You lying!" she yelled.

"If I'm lying I'm flying!" I said to her.

"Well, come show me please!" she screamed in my ear.

"Text me the address so I can throw it my GPS system," I told her and hung up. A few minutes later, I got the message, so I hopped in the shower.

I had to be cute in my new car. It's pretty warm now, so I chose some Seven jeans with a black belt and a white cropped top shirt that said "Being bad makes good stories" and I headed out of the door.

I was speeding, so I got there in no time. Lexis met me outside and ran to the car screaming! She was more excited than I was for me, which is why she is my best friend. She's far from a hater and she's always genuinely happy for people. She hugged me while she jumped, before we walked inside. Frankie and some chick were sitting in the living room. The chick was thick and cute and made me wonder if she was there for Frankie or the asshole. Which reminded me that he lives here! Ugh!

"Why were y'all screaming?" Frankie asked.

"None of your business." Alexis answered, which caused Frankie to roll her eyes and me to chuckle.

"I was showing her my new car." I beamed with joy.

"Oh ok. Congratulations," she said and Alexis' jaw dropped.

"What?" I asked her.

"She been a total bitch to me since I met her but she's being nice to you!" she said.

"That's because I ain't fucking the man she loves," I said to Alexis, which caused her and Frankie to gasp at the same time. I started laughing and the other chick was just sitting there, watching and waiting for some shit to pop off.

"What are you saying?" Alexis asked me.

"I'm saying anybody with eyes or anybody paying attention can tell she's in love with Phat. That's why she don't like you. I'm guessing she's never liked anybody he's ever messed with." I said simply.

"I love Phat like a brother," Frankie said, in a matter of fact tone.

"You love your brothers like that?" I asked her with my face turned up at her and the other chick started to laugh.

"Your cab ain't here yet Brittany?" Frankie asked her with an attitude. I straightened up at the sound of her name.

"You here for Chris?" I asked her.

"Yes. That's my man," she said.

"Yo man making you catch a cab?" I asked and chuckled. She stood up to approach me and I waited until she got within arms reached before I stood as well.

I didn't give her a chance to say anything because I slid my hand into my pocket where I kept my brass knuckles and punched her in the face. She fell on the floor as I slid my hand back in my pocket to remove it. "This ain't what you want sweetie. Instead of taking your anger out on me, you should try going back there to take it out on the nigga that fucked you and told you to catch a cab. He should have at least had the cab out there waiting on you," I said laughing.

"What the hell y'all in here doing?" someone asked, which caused us to look down the hall. Frankie rolled her eyes and I looked away quickly when I saw Chris' sexy chocolate body walking down the hall with just his boxers on. Nobody answered him. "Nessa, what you doing here?" he asked me.

"I'm here with Lexis. Should I leave?" I asked him.

"No but can I holla at you real quick?" he asked me.

"Nope," I replied and sat down.

"So, you don't see me right here?" Brittany asked him from the floor.

"Damn, the cab ain't came yet? Why the fuck you on the floor? Your nose bleeding?" he asked and shook his head with disgust all over his face.

"She tried to fight me," I answered for her. His face went from disgust to anger in a matter of seconds.

"Get the fuck out!" he said. I didn't know who he was talking to. He walked over to us, snatched Brittany up off the floor, and walked her to the door. "Flag a cab down," he told her and pushed her outside.

"Can we talk?" he asked, as he walked back into the living room.

"No," I replied.

"Nessa."

"No"

"Man-"

"No!" I said firmly.

"Fuck it," he said before going back to the back.

"Girl, he ain't never did that before!" Frankie said.

"What?" I asked.

"He practically begging you to talk to him!" she said. I looked over at Alexis, who was sitting back smiling. I shrugged my shoulders before I sat back in my chair.

I didn't realize how tired I was until I woke up in a bed. I got so fucking scared, I flung the covers off me and jumped out of it and looked around. I heard a light chuckle, which caused me to jump around and back pedal until I realized it was Chris, who was laughing. "What the hell did you do to me?" I asked him and he shook his head.

I turned and headed towards the door, "I'm sorry," Chris said and stopped me dead in my tracks. C'mon now, who expects an asshole to apologize for anything?

"Apology accepted," I replied and opened the door.

"Wait," he said.

"Let's not make this more than it has to be. You apologized and I accepted it. It's over with," I said over my shoulder as I headed out the door. I walked around the living room as I looked for my things but couldn't find them anywhere.

Frankie was asleep in the same spot she was in when I got here. "Hey, have you seen my things?" I asked as I lightly shook her awake.

"Mmmhhhh," she responded. I shook her a bit harder and she jumped up and swung wildly. I took a step back before I side kicked her back in the chair.

"Do you always show up to people's houses kicking them out of their sleep?" she asked.

"Have you seen my things?" I asked, ignoring her question because I could have done a lot more than kick her and I would have had one of those licks connected.

"Chris grabbed you and all of your things when he carried you in his room," she answered, which caused me to shake my head. That's probably why he didn't follow me out. He's such a fucking asshole for this.

"Can you go back there and get them for me?" I asked her.

She stood up and stretched and yawned before she headed towards Chris' room.

"Get the fuck out my room Frankie! She can get her own shit!" I heard Chris yell, loud enough for me to hear. She came back down the hall and shrugged her shoulders before she sat back in her spot.

"Do you have a room?" I asked her because I only counted three bedrooms and she's always out here.

"Yes. Phat, Chris, and I have our own rooms. James and Steve crash out here on the couch or in one of our rooms on the couch bed," she answered.

"If everybody's grown, why don't y'all just get y'all own spots?" I asked her and she answered with a shrug of the shoulder. They probably wouldn't know how to make it without the other one. I just know I'd get tired of waking up in a house with this many people every day. It would be different if they had a house with five bedrooms and everyone had their own space but this apartment only has three bedrooms. It just can't be comfortable.

I shook my head and walked towards the back, not really remembering where I came from. I opened the door and shocked my damn self! Phat was sitting on the bed with his back against the headboard and his eyes were closed. Alexis was riding him backwards moaning like crazy, as Phat twisted her nipples with both hands. I stood there and watched them, unable to move. Both of their eyes were closed, so they didn't know I was standing there.

For the first time ever, my pussy started to feel weird. I knew it was because I wanted to feel exactly how Alexis was feeling at this moment. All of a sudden, a hand covered my mouth and the door closed. "Enjoying the show?" he asked. I turned around to Steve standing there looking at me all creepy like. "I can take you to my room and do that to you," he said and grabbed his dick through his pants.

"What room? Get your own room before you holla at me and even when you get it, don't holla at me," I replied as I walked off.

As I was walking back towards the front of the apartment, I noticed a room door was open. As I glanced in, I saw Chris stretched out across the bed, knocked out. I stopped in the door, doing a quick sweep across the room with my eyes and spotted my things on the nightstand next to the bed. I walked slowly towards it, hoping to sneak in and out without waking him up. A slow smile spread across my face, once I was able to grab my things without waking him up. I was closing in on the door when it closed and my purse was snatched out of my grasp.

"What the fuck Chris?" I asked, clearly annoyed. "You're not leaving until we talk," he stated as he headed back to his bed. I followed behind him and waited on him to start talking. He sat on his bed against the headboard, and made me think of Phat and Alexis and I felt that feeling between my legs again. "What do you want to talk about and why?" I asked him and he answered with a shrug.

"How's your birthday going?" he asked and patted the spot in front of him.

"I'm not getting on this nasty bed you just fucked someone in!" I said with my lip turned up at him.

"I fucked her over there," he said and pointed towards the couch. "I only fuck on the couch," he continued, still patting the spot in front of him. I reluctantly crawled on the bed in front of him.

"Man, take your damn shoes off in my bed girl!" he demanded as I slid out of them. "So?" he asked.

"So what?"

"How's your birthday going girl?" he asked with a slight attitude.

"It'd be better if I didn't feel like a prisoner!" I answered with an attitude. I really wanted to tell him that I was enjoying this cat and mouse game we've been playing all day. I really wanted to ask him how he felt about me but of course, I was too afraid to say any of those things.

"Let's watch TV," he said and handed me the remote. I turned the station to ABC and Pretty Little Liars was just starting. "Man, that song creepy as fuck girl. What you got me watching?" he asked with a laugh.

"It's kind of hard to explain, you'd just have to watch it from the beginning," I responded.

"Is it on Netflix?"

"Yea." He grabbed the remote and switched it to Netflix. He then searched the show and played episode one of season one. That totally shocked the fuck out of me because most guys don't want to watch this show. Most guys won't even give it a try, yet here he is, willing to watch it with me and I didn't even tell him what it's about.

We sat on the bed watching Pretty Little Liars when he grabbed my shoulders and gave them a strong massage. "Mmmmhhh," I moaned as I lowered my head.

"Want me to massage your back, birthday girl?" he asked as I nodded my head. "Take your shirt off," he said as I gave him a questioning look. He reached in his nightstand and pulled massage oil out "Take your shirt off," he said again. I stood up and took my shirt and jeans off because I wanted him to give me a full body massage.

Chris Butler

Vanessa's ass got me doing shit I don't normally do for these bitches. I was so shocked she came back. I didn't know what to do. I hopped out of the shower and thought I was tripping when I heard her voice, so I dove on my bed chilling. Then I was like what the fuck is going on because they were making a lot of noise in the living room.

Imagine my surprise when I walk in and see Frankie, Alexis, and Vanessa chilling. It took a minute for me to see Brittany was still there and I wasn't going to acknowledge her, but she wanted to be seen. She was sitting on the floor with her nose bleeding and shit, looking stupid as fuck! Bitches that want that much attention be killing me. Knowing her, the cab done been here and left, and she just want me to take her home. That shit ain't happening though.

I got so fucking mad when Vanessa told me she tried to fight her that I kicked her ass out! I don't even know what made me so mad since Vanessa and I just met today, and we ain't together or trying to be but shit, it's something about her. Her little ass had me in the living room begging her to come talk to me. When I realized what I was doing, I just walked back into my room.

I laid across my bed about an hour watching TV but I kept thinking about Vanessa. About thirty minutes later, I decided to try my luck with talking to her again. When I walked in the living room, she was knocked out and Frankie was watching TV. I noticed Frankie hadn't looked at me since she saw my dick earlier today and the look on her face made me chuckle a bit to myself. I grabbed her phone and keys, dropped them in her purse, and took it in my room. I came back, swept her little ass up in my arms, and carried her to my bed.

Shocking my damn self, I tucked her in. See what I mean? She got me doing shit I've never thought to do but with her it comes natural. Laying her on the couch didn't even cross my mind because I can tell she's better than that.

After tucking her in, I sat on the couch and watched her sleep. I noticed she doesn't close her eyes completely and that shit is kind of scary! She doesn't snore though, so that's a good sign. Her ass must be really tired because I started dozing off before she woke up. You should have seen her sitting up and looking everywhere but over here! Had she looked over here, she wouldn't have been so spooked. Then she hopped out the bed about to haul ass before I started laughing at her.

Her fear went away but I could cut the tension that filled the room with a knife! I tried apologizing and she still walked out on me, so I don't know what else to do. She probably thought I was going to chase her but she wasn't going anywhere without her shit, so she would have to come back in here.

A few minutes later, Frankie brought her ass to my door! I knew what she wanted before she opened her mouth. I see Vanessa thinks she's slick but I'm slicker. I sent Frankie on her way loud enough for smart ass to know she had to come her damn self. I didn't count on Frankie's dumb ass to close the door to my room though. I had a feeling she wouldn't know where she came from because I don't think she pays much attention to her surroundings. I heard footsteps passing my door and figuring it was her as I got up to open the door. I saw her open Phat's door and she was standing there like they were talking to her or something. Steve walked out of Frankie's room and right up on her, covering her mouth and closing Phat's door. They must have been fucking, so Vanessa gotta be a freak to be standing there watching them, right?

My blood began to boil as I watched them talk about fucking. Ok, I'm over exaggerating. He was trying to fuck and she put him in his place. Yet, she calls me an asshole. I laid across my bed, closing my eyes so she would think I was asleep. I could hear her heavy foot ass walking slow and I could hear her breathing. It took everything in me not to laugh at her. Common sense should have told her I didn't fall asleep that damn fast! Hell, it hadn't even been ten minutes since she sent Frankie back here. I waited until she was close to the door before creeping up on her, closing it, and snatching her purse.

She got so mad and I thought it was funny. I normally don't try this hard but like I said, it's something about her. It took a minute to get her close enough to me to try my hand with her. Of course, I'm going to try to fuck her. I mean, who wouldn't?

I was pulling out all of the stops tonight to get a feel of her. I'm already digging her and if the pussy good, I'm going to keep her. I gave her the remote so she can pick us something out to watch and she picked some show about four teenage girls, and I was actually interested in it. What caught my attention was the theme song! I was staring at Vanessa from behind her when it started playing:

> *Got a secret*
> *Can you keep it?*
> *Swear this one you'll save*
> *Better lock it in your pocket*
> *Taking this one to the grave*
> *If I show you then I know you won't tell what I said*
> *'Cause two can keep a secret if one of them is dead*

I was looking so damn crazy because that's one way to catch a nigga's attention. I tried to get her to tell me what it was about but she kind of suggested I watch it from the beginning.

I was honestly going to try and pay attention but this is the first time I've ever had a bitch in my bed. I normally bring bitches in, fuck them on the couch, and put they asses out. The face she made when I wanted her to get in the bed with me was hilarious. I didn't laugh though because I wanted her up here with me. She's going to be the only bitch I fuck in this bed too.

I didn't really know how to get her naked because we just met this morning and she doesn't seem like the type of bitch to take her clothes off just because I told her to. I had to take it way back to school days and give her a massage. I started massaging her shoulders and when she let out that moan, my dick started coming alive.

She obliged to having a back massage but she got her ass up and took everything off except her bra and panties. That means she wants to fuck, right? What female does that for a massage? Hell, I was really expecting her to snap on me when I told her to take her shirt off. Now I'm second guessing doing this on my bed. Shit, any bitch that will get naked like that need to be on the couch! It's too late now though because if I tell her to go over there, I know she gone snap because she knows Brittany was just there.

I watched her lay across my bed and started watching TV. I had to take a moment to admire her tone slim body. I don't think she works out or anything, so I wonder how she keeps it tight like this. I slowly squeezed the massage oil into the palm of my hand before rubbing them together. I started on her neck and moved slowly but firmly to her shoulders. "Mmmmmhhh," she moaned softly. I had to adjust myself because I was straddling her and didn't want her to feel what her moans were doing to my dick. Well, not this soon anyway.

Knock, Knock

"Noo. Don't stop," she moaned and I had to stop because my shit was rock hard after that.

"I'll be right back Nessa," I said, as I leaned down and whispered in her ear. I adjusted my dick again on my way to answer the door.

"Yo! We about to go to Applebee's and grab a to-go box, do y'all want something?" Phat asked. I was about to say no but Vanessa yelled that she wanted twenty boneless wings and Alexis started laughing.

"I'll eat with her," I said.

"No the fuck you want!" she fired back, which caused Alexis to laugh harder.

"She don't share food and will punch you if you touch her food. Y'all gone be in there fighting," Alexis said and caused me and Phat to laugh at her.

"Well, bring me a steak well done and mashed potatoes," I said.

"Iight, bet," Phat said. He gave me dap and walked away.

"Don't be in there trying to fuck my friend already!" Alexis said before she walked away. I just shook my head, hoping Vanessa didn't hear her.

Walking back towards the bed, I sat next to her as she laid there watching this Pretty Little Liars show. She looked so comfortable and at home, like she belonged here with me. "What you doing boy?!" she asked with a slight attitude.

"What you mean? I ain't did shit!" I said confused.

"Exactly! You spose to be giving me a massage! Hurry up before they come back with the food," she said, which caused me to laugh. I grabbed the massage oil and moved down to her back. I rubbed the oil all over her back before I moved her arms from her sides to over her head. I massaged slow deep circles all over her upper and lower back and inched my way closer to her sides.

"Mmmmhh. Let me find out," she said seductively, which caused me to chuckle a little bit. Vanessa is truly something else with herself right now. I slid my body down, so I could massage her thighs. I applied more oil and started massaging deeply, occasionally bumping her pussy. Surprisingly, I was able to control myself and she couldn't feel my dick growing because of the way I was positioned. I could feel the heat coming from her pussy, which made me bump it some more just so I could touch it.

I grabbed one thigh and kneaded it with my fingertips when she moved the other one over, which gave me better access to touch her. Bitch thinks she's slick! Now that I know she wants me to touch it, I'm not going to unless she asked me to do it. I could see that it was bare and smooth looking because when she moved her leg, her panties shifted and gave me a pretty good view. I switched thighs and massaged as close to her pussy as I could without actually touching it. She moaned softly the entire time. I moved down to her lower leg, then feet and when I looked at her pussy, I could see it glistening. She laid completely still with her eyes closed as she moaned softly.

I climbed back on the bed slowly and debated on what I should do next. I couldn't resist that pretty pink pussy and I've never put my mouth on one before because the shit just seemed unsafe. It felt like the thing to do right now.

I inched closer to her, blew lightly on her pussy, and watched as her body shook lightly and she moaned softly. I slid my tongue and stiffened it, so it could feel like I'm tongue fucking her. Her pussy juices were so sweet and it made me wonder if I've been missing out all of these by not reciprocating the oral love. I sucked lightly on her clit, which caused her to moan louder, then I blew softly on it. I didn't have a clue what I was doing but I bet you couldn't pay Vanessa to believe I'd never done this before. I moved her panties to the side to give me better access and dove back in. I sucked on her clit more aggressively and she squirmed, like she was running away from me. I locked her legs down with my arms to keep her still because she was getting her pussy juices all over my damn face!

"Ooooh Chris! What are you doing to me?" she moaned out.

"Aw. Fuck! It feels so good!" she continued.

"Well, why you running?" I asked before I sucked harder on her clit.

"Awww stop! Chris stop! I gotta pee! Stop!" she said and pulled away from again. I didn't let her go because I knew she was about to nut, not piss. I sucked harder as her body started to shake and her juices spilled out as I lapped her sweet nectar up like she was my last meal.

Vanessa Broughton

Knock, knock

"Mmmhhh," I groaned and stirred in my sleep.

"What you do to her?" I heard Alexis asking.

"I ain't do shit to her, she sleep!" Chris responded.

"Move out my way." I heard Alexis say, then Chris laughed at her. A few seconds later I could feel her shaking me.

"Stop Lex. I'm tired," I said and pushed her hands off me.

"What did he do to you?" she asked with concern evident in her voice.

It was then that I started to think about the way he just made my body feel. I was still riding the waves of Chris' tongue. You thought I was digging him before but it just got worse.

"Are you ok?" Alexis asked, which brought me back to reality.

"Yes," I answered with my eyes still closed.

"I got your food," she said and I jumped up, which caused her, Phat, and Chris to all laugh at me.

I personally don't find a damn thing funny about them having my food since I was starving! "Where is it?" I asked Alexis.

"Up front. Chris doesn't let anyone eat in his room," she said and stood up.

"Bull! I'm about to go get my food and come back to finish Pretty Little Liars!" I said and walked past them.

"Man, no the fuck you ain't! I don't eat in my own damn room!" Chris yelled behind my back.

"Liar! You just ate in there!" I fired back with a smirk as I made my way into the kitchen. I grabbed my plate and headed back to Chris' room. "Move!" I said to Chris because he was blocking me from entering.

"Naw man, you ain't fina have bbq sauce all over my shit!" he said with the sexiest scowl I've ever seen on his face. I walked as close to him as I possibly could and stood on the tips of my toes. I grabbed his face and made him bend over, so I could kiss his lips. He hesitated at first but a few seconds in, he was tonguing me down. I pulled away and sucked his bottom lip before I passed him to go inside his room. I crawled on the bed to finish watching Pretty Little Liars. When I looked at the door, he was still standing there. You could see the attitude all over his face.

"Um... excuse me miss thang! When you start doing that?" Alexis asked with her hands on her hips.

"It's a first time for everything," I responded with a shrug.

"Did y'all...?" she trailed off with her mouth wide open and looked between the two of us.

"I ain't fuck her man," Chris said.

"Damn, she ain't give up the pussy and she got you stuck on stupid already?" Phat asked and laughed. I looked over at Chris, who had an unreadable expression on his face.

"Man, get the fuck out my room!" he said to Alexis and Phat, which caused them to laugh on their way out of the door.

He walked over to me and I didn't know if I should run or act like I didn't see the mean mug on his face. Since I had already opened my food, I decided to ignore him. He stood next to the bed and I could feel him mugging me. All of a sudden, he grabbed my food and headed for the door.

See, he must didn't believe Alexis because I promise, one thing I don't play about is my food! I hopped up and ran behind him and pushed the door back closed. "Give me my food!" I screamed at him.

"Naw, you can take ya lil fat ass in the kitchen and eat like I said!" he screamed back in my face. The only reason I didn't hit him is because he had my food in his hand. Rest assure when he sit my shit down, I'm going to molly wop his ass!

He stormed out of the room and headed towards the kitchen. I was so mad my armpits and chest itched. I glanced in the living room and saw that everyone else was sitting down eating and watching TV. Well, they were until we came in and now, they were about to get a show. "I knew he wasn't gone let her eat in his room," Phat said, just as Chris slammed my take out box on the kitchen counter.

"Now, eat in here with ever-"

I cut Chris off as my fist connected with his jaw. "Don't touch my fucking food ever! Especially when I'm eating!" I screamed in his face.

"I knew she wasn't going to let that slide," Alexis to Phat. I couldn't believe they were just sitting there talking about it like it wasn't happening currently.

I turned to look at them but Chris pushed my head so hard that I stumbled back into the living room until I caught my balance. "What the fuck Chris?" Alexis asked and tried to jump up but Phat grabbed her around the waist.

"Don't put your hands on me and I won't put mine on you!" Chris said before he walked back through the living room.

"Don't do it." I heard Alexis say to me. I hopped up and ran full speed at Chris down the hall. I slid between his legs just as he was turning to hit me. I punched him as hard as I could in his nuts on my way under him.

"Bitch!" he yelled and dropped to his knees in the hallway.

"Dayyummm!" I heard someone say in the living room.

I stepped over him and headed back in the kitchen to get my food. When I walked out, Alexis and Phat had the same worried expression on their faces. I walked back down the hall, stepped over Chris, and headed back in his room.

I wasn't in there ten minutes before Chris walked in and slammed the door closed behind him. I could hear Alexis and Phat arguing but I couldn't hear exactly what they were saying. He walked up to me and glared before he grabbed my plate and sat it on his nightstand. Before I could say anything, he cocked back and slapped me so hard, I flipped off the bed and landed on my back. It took me a minute to catch my breath, so I think he knocked the wind out of me. I could feel my face swelling almost immediately.

I laid on the floor in shock and tried to catch my breath as Chris limped his way to me. "Nobody eats in my room, do you understand?" he asked, as he leaned over me. I just stared at him with tears welled up in my eyes. I could feel a lump starting to form in my throat. I wanted to cry so bad but I refuse to let him see me down. I swallowed hard, took a deep breath, and spin kicked with all of my might and swept him off his feet. I jumped to a standing position and sat on his chest, and punched him as hard as I could in his face. Normally, I would have been pulled my brass knuckles out but I didn't want to with him.

I lost count of how many times I punched him. All I know is his mouth and nose were bleeding. He grabbed my thighs and lifted me in the air before he threw me across the room. When I hit the floor, I slid and hit the dresser, which caused the top two drawers to fall out. I was able to knock one away from my head but I wasn't fast enough to knock the other one away. The room started to spin, then everything went black.

Chris Butler

I know what you're thinking but you can save that shit! I don't give a fuck how much bigger than Vanessa I am or the fact that she's female because the bitch hit me! I'll never hit a woman but I'll knock a bitch out! I promise I wouldn't have touched her if she wouldn't have hit me in my face. It's bad enough the bitch hit like a man, so fuck what you thought! Let her little ass hit you like that and see what the fuck you do!

The bitch just refused to eat in the kitchen. I don't understand that part at all because everybody else was in the living room eating. If she wanted to watch TV and eat, she could have eaten in the living room. She was just determined to eat in my damn bed! It wouldn't have been a big deal had she sat on the couch but no, she wants to eat in my bed! I didn't want my room smelling like food and I didn't want crumbs in my bed. I don't care how neat you think you eat; you will leave some crumbs behind.

When she punched me in my dick, I thought I was gone die! I felt my nuts go in my stomach and I almost threw up all over the hall floor. How could I not slap fire from her hot ass? Man, I walked in the room trying to talk myself out of it but the more I looked at her sitting on my bed eating, the more logical slapping her seemed. She flipped off my bed after I hit her, so I decided to tell her one more time. "Nobody eats in my room; do you understand?" I asked her just to make sure we were finally on the same page.

She looked at me like she wanted to kill me. I felt bad when I noticed her face was red and swelling until this bitch tripped me from her position on the floor! My first thought was *Where did this bitch learn this from?* But before I could process the thought, she was on me, punching me in the face. My vision started to become cloudy, so I knew my shit was swelling up. I could feel the blood sliding down my face but I didn't know where it was coming from. When I started to feel lightheaded I knew I had to get the lil bitch off me, so I threw her.

I laid completely still trying to stop the room from spinning. She did a number on me and I really took it easy on her because she's a female. I could have easily fucked her up but I wasn't trying to kill her and that's what would have happened. I stayed on the floor for about ten minutes before I realized she didn't get up swinging. The way she was banging a nigga, I just knew she would be back over here and fight me again.

I sat up slowly because my head was killing me. I walked in the bathroom to look at my face and couldn't believe how bad this bitch had done fucked me up. I'm 5'9" and I weigh about 220lbs., and it looked like I got in a fight with a man my size! My right eye was swollen, my nose was broken, and my bottom lip was split open on the right side. I just shook my head and took an Advil out of my medicine cabinet.

I walked out into the hallway to get a clean towel and came back to wash my face. The shit hurt so fucking bad. I didn't know if I should just deal with it or go to the hospital.

When I walked back out of my bathroom, I noticed she was still on the floor. I started to leave her little ass there but what I did was bad enough already. I walked closer to her and noticed her chest was rising and falling, so I knew she was still breathing. The dresser's drawer must have knocked her out. I grabbed my clothes and placed them back in the drawers before sliding the drawers back into the dresser.

After I straightened up, I ran her a hot bath because I knew she would be sore when she got up. I carefully removed all of her clothes until her toned body was completely naked. I placed her in the water thinking she would wake up as soon as she felt it. I walked out and grabbed another towel and when I came back in the bathroom, she was still out. I gently cleaned her face before bathing her from head to toe. I walked out, letting her soak a little longer before taking her out.

I grabbed her food, taking it back into the kitchen with all eyes on me. They didn't see my face until I was walking out of the kitchen and everybody's mouths dropped. "Damn bruh, you good?" Phat asked as I nodded my head.

"I think that lip need stitches. I can see it's open from over here. Where's Nessa?" Alexis asked.

"Frankie, I need you to wash my stuff, so Nessa can have something clean to put on when she wakes up." I said to Frankie, ignoring Alexis.

"What you mean 'wake up'? What you do to her?" Alexis asked, standing to her feet but Phat grabbed her. "What you do to her?!" she screamed with tears streaming down her face trying to get to me. "Let me go Phat! He hurt my friend for nothing!" she screamed at him, still crying. He shook his head at me while holding on to her tighter, as she cried in her arms.

"I ain't hurt the bitch for nothing. Did y'all not see her hit me? Do you not see my fucking face right now? Fuck hurting, she's lucky I didn't kill her!" I said snapping on Alexis, who only cried harder. "All she had to do was come in here and eat but she wanted to sit in my room on my bed like something's wrong with her! Frankie, what the fuck you waiting on?!" I screamed, causing Frankie to jump and do as she was told.

Alexis wiped her tears and stared at me like she wanted to kill me. "Every single day growing up, they ate at the table together as a family. Every day for eight years until her mother died, they ate together in the kitchen! Now, she can't. Had she eaten in the kitchen or even in here with us, she would have broken down! She eats in the room watching TV because that's the only thing she can do that's not something she did with her mother," Alexis said through clenched teeth.

Now I felt like shit but I didn't know any of that shit. I knew her mom was dead but I didn't know anything specific. "That still don't justify the bitch hitting me," I said as I looked Alexis square in the eyes.

"Well, I told you how she was about her food," she said before she sat down with Phat.

I walked back down the hall into the room to check on her and she was still out. I scooped her up and laid her across my bed before I grabbed a dry off towel and dried her off. I grabbed the massage oil and rubbed it on her legs and arms before putting one of my shirts on her and some boxers. I tucked her in and left out of the room and headed straight out of the door.

"Where you going bruh?" Phat asked me.

"Out," I replied and closed the door behind me. I walked around with my lip split open for about thirty minutes before I ended up at Walmart. Everybody was looking at me crazy and I was flipping all of them bitches the bird. I ended up by the kitchen ware and saw a tray used for eating in the bed. It was

$45, I bought it and headed back to the crib. When I got close, I stopped to get some wrapping paper and let the store clerk wrap it up for me.

When I walked back in the house, Frankie and Phat were watching TV in the living room. "I wouldn't go back there if I were you," Frankie said.

"That's why you're Frankie," I replied and walked into the kitchen. I warmed Vanessa's wings up and carried them in the room with her.

Vanessa was sitting in my bed with ice on her head and Alexis was standing next to the bed as she rubbed her hair. When they noticed I had entered the room, they both shot me evil glares, like they wanted me out. "Get out Alexis," I said to her.

"No. I'm not leaving so you can kill her," she replied and folded her arms across her chest.

"C'mon girl. Mind your business," Phat said, appearing out of nowhere. Alexis turned around and kissed Vanessa on the forehead before she followed Phat out of the room.

"Why you closing the door? You want to fight some more?" Vanessa asked as she leaned back on the headboard.

"I got you something," I said as I ignored her and handed her the box. I watched as she opened it and tears started falling down her cheeks. I'm glad Alexis told me about her mom, but I wish I had known before all of this went down because I still wanted to get to know her and now, I don't know if that chance is still there. After she opened it completely, I handed her her wings and she dug in without saying another word.

I waited until she was finished to apologize to her and she just nodded her head. "Where are my clothes? What time is it?" she asked.

"Frankie is washing them and it's almost 2am," I answered.

"Oh fuck, I gotta go home." she said and tried to get up.

Noticing she was in pain, I grabbed her and sat her back on the bed. "Man, you ain't driving nowhere like this. Lay yo ass down!" I screamed at her and surprisingly, she listened to me.

I hopped in the shower and laid down with her falling into a deep sleep. I had never slept that hard in my life, so I know I need Vanessa by my side. I just hope she gives me a chance. When I woke up alone in the bed, I didn't know what to think.

Vanessa Broughton

I woke up in so much pain I could barely move. I could feel the side of my face was swollen and I had a knot on my head. I felt like a damn crash test dummy as I cried silently. I couldn't believe I fought a man and he fought me back. I use to watch shows on TV and get mad when women hit men, expecting them not to retaliate. I guess I didn't expect him not to. I just didn't expect him to go so hard with it.

What confused me was him kicking my ass then bathing me and putting me to bed. The same bed he slapped me out of. Even through all of that, I still wanted him. Now, how dumb is that? I still wanted to try but trust me, I'm no dummy. I know that if he will hit you once then he will hit you twice and pretty soon, all he'll be doing is hitting you.

I looked over at the couch half hoping he would be sitting there but Alexis was. I sat all the way up and leaned back against the headboard for support and groaned loudly from the pain. The noises I was making caused Alexis to hop up, run over to me, and wrap her arms around me. "Are you ok?" she asked as I nodded my head. "Bitch, you fucked him up!" she exclaimed as I looked at her confused.

"Shit, I'm the one fucked up! My head is killing me!" I said to her. She handed me two pills and a glass of water.

"Bitch, your head hurt but your nose ain't broken and your lip ain't split open," she said and my jaw dropped. I didn't remember doing all of that to him. As a matter of fact, I didn't use any weapons so I wouldn't do that to him.

"Is he ok?" I asked her as she nodded her head with a frown.

"His ass left after he snapped on me. Don't get mad but I told him why you wanted to eat in here," she said and I looked away.

Memories filled my head of the times we ate together as a family. Every morning we ate breakfast together and every evening we ate dinner together. Even on game day during football season, we still ate together. We just migrated into the living room. We would sit around telling my mom about our plans for the day during breakfast and how our days went during dinner. I could feel the lump forming in throat and my eyes began to burn from the tears. I didn't try to stop it or hold back because this was Alexis. I could totally be me without judgement in front of her, and I am so thankful for her. I cried on her shoulder as she hugged me.

It took a few minutes for me to stop but I was able to pull myself together. She helped me to the bathroom to wash my face and then back to the bed. I was so fucking dizzy; I didn't know what to do. We sat there and talked until the devil made his way back into the room putting Alexis out.

After she left, he gave me a gift. When I opened the bedside tray, I could feel the waterworks beginning and I swear I felt like the biggest punk ever! He even let me eat my food in his room and I could feel him staring at me the whole time. He apologized after I finished and I didn't even want to talk about it. I just wanted to go home and get in my own bed and do normal shit like shoot squirrels and birds from my bedroom window without arguing or fighting anyone.

After he told me it was damn near 2 o'clock in the morning, I was really ready to go but the pain was too much to bear. I was so happy when he made me get back in the bed, that's why I didn't fight with him. I laid in his arms and fell asleep, literally feeling like this is where I belonged.

When I woke up, I noticed he was still asleep and my things were on his dresser. I slid out of his arms, got dressed, grabbed my things, and headed home. For some reason, it was extremely hard to leave him. Probably because I knew that was the end of us and it had barely begun. Hopefully getting over him wouldn't be as hard as my mind was telling me it was going to be. After all, I had just met him yesterday. I guess it was love at first sight for me, well love when I first noticed him.

As I walked into the house, I could hear the TV in the living room was on, which let me know that Wayne was up and waiting on me to come home. I honestly don't know why we still all live together when we are all adults! I'm 24 years old and Wayne is 28 years old, so it's about damn time that we get our own spot. My problem is I don't have a job and the only thing I know how to do is kill.

"Where have you been?" Wayne asked as I was passing by the living room.

"Minding," I answered and headed towards my room.

"Vanessa, I have been worried sick about you! Don't you ever not come home again! Do you understand me?" Wayne screamed at me, which caused me to turn around with an attitude.

"Wayne, I am grown! I'm 24 years old and I'm tired of you treating me like a fucking child! I'm going to get a job and I'm going to move the fuck outta here!" I screamed back. If he was that damned worried, he would have called or texted or something but he ain't do none of that shit.

"What the hell happened to your face?" he asked as he approached me, clearly ignoring everything that I just said to him.

"Get away from me. I fell," I stated as I turned around.

I walked in my room to change into workout clothes, so I could go for a run. I only run when I need to clear my mind and figure things out. I haven't had to run in years and I know that I'm only running now because of Chris and my need to be on my own. I was dressed and back out the door in no time.

As I ran around the block, my foggy mind began to clear up. I needed to get out of this controlling house but in order to do that, I need to make money. The only thing I can do is kill people, so why not get people to pay me for that. I slowed my pace when I noticed I was approaching a newspaper stand. "Hey, excuse me. How much for an ad in the business section?" I asked the man who was selling papers.

"$35. Here's the card with the number on it to purchase one when you're ready," he answered me.

"Thanks!" I yelled and jogged off with a smile on my face.

Now, I just need to figure out how I can inconspicuously post an ad and market my services without being too obvious.

As soon as I got home, I realized I had left my phone here and when I checked it, I had four missed calls and a few messages from Alexis. I'm going to have to call her back later because right now, I have to think of a way to post this ad without giving myself away. I still have my old Tracfone, so I can use that number because it can't be traced back to me. Maybe I can charge 2500 dollars for men and 4500 for women. Once I get my name out there, I'd be able to charge a bit more.

I laid back in my bed thinking of ways to word my ad, so people would call me for jobs. After hours of deliberation and no help at all, I had finally figured out what I wanted my ad to say. The next morning, I used my Tracfone to call the number on the card the newspaper salesman gave me to place my ad.

"Good morning. This is Angela with the New York Timesout! How may I help you?" Angela said when she answered the phone. I immediately hung the phone up. If anything went south, Angela would be able to identify me with a voice line up. Fuck! Now what do I do?

"Hello," I answered my phone without looking.

"Why'd you leave?" the voice said, which caused me to pull the phone away from my ear to look at the screen. It said Alexis but I knew at this point, it was Chris. As happy as I was that he reached out to me, I knew we could never be. Things got too physical for us to ever get past that. I've never been in a relationship before but I watch the fuck out of the Lifetime Movie Network and it never gets better.

"I didn't want to be around you any longer than I needed to be. I'd appreciate it if you never contacted me again," I said and hung up the phone.

Ok, I know that I sounded like an asshole but I had to say exactly what I meant, so he wouldn't twist my words to mean something else and end up trying again at a later date. I'm positive that if I would have given him another chance to be whatever it was he was trying to be; the abuse would have continued. I know I started the physical part but he didn't have to slap me as hard as he did, knocking me off the bed. I'm 5'4" and 130 lbs., so he needs to know his strength!

Anyway, I can't dwell on that when it's money to be made. All I need to do is find a smoker that will place the call for the ad for me and pay with this prepaid debit card I got. I activated it under the alias Princess Diamond. I needed to make some moves fast, so I got up, hopped in the shower, and got dressed.

"Where you going?" Wayne asked as I was walking out of the front door.

"Out. Why?" I asked him.

"Are you ok sis?" Wayne asked me.

"Just peachy!" I yelled over my shoulder as I closed the door. I hopped in my car and prepared for the long ride to Newark.

I found some run down projects and drove through them before I parked at the convenient store on the corner. I touched my sides to make sure my throwing stars were secure and in place. I could feel my knife was still in place at my ankle but my bootleg jeans concealed it.

I hopped out of the car and looked around to make sure it was safe to continue. I'm not from here and people have been killed for less. I noticed there were guys shooting dice on the side of the building and one, in particular, caught my attention. He was brown skinned with his hair cut low. He looked edible and I wanted him to do me the same way Chris did me on my birthday! This guy had this aura that surrounded him and commanded attention and baby, he had mine!

I stood there and watched them shoot dice, noticing how everybody was calling everybody but him a bitch. I could tell they respected him and if I had a body like Alexis, he would have already looked at me by now.

I continued to scope the scenery and noticed the smokers lingering around the third project house on the left. I began my journey into the projects and surprisingly, there were cat calls being made. A lot of the guys were trying to get my attention but now isn't the time. I have to remain focused, so I can get this part of my plan out of the way and start on my next one.

Can you imagine my surprise when a smoker approached me? Man, I was walking slow as fuck, trying to figure out how I could get one to trust me enough to talk to me being as though I'm not from these parts. "Got a dollar?" the smoker asked me.

I took a moment to take her in, so I would remember her face. She was shorter and smaller than me and it looked like she was once a beautiful woman. She had light skin with dark blotches all over her body. "What's your name?" I asked her.

"Kim. Got a dollar?" she responded.

I noticed all of her teeth were rotted out. I wanted to call the bitch 'young gummy' but I needed her to help me. "I got ten, if you do me a favor," I said to her and watched her eyes light up.

"Name it," she said, keeping it short with me.

"I want you to call this number and tell her what you want the newspaper ad to say and pay with this card," I said as I handed her the note I wrote, which had what I wanted the ad say. She stared at it strangely, which made me wonder if she could read.

"Why can't you do it yaself?" she asked me and gave me the side eye.

"I just get nervous when talking to people," I answered and handed her the phone.

I watched as she called the number and asked if she could purchase an ad over the phone. "Yes, I have a card. Uh, business. Need a job done but can't get your hands dirty? Call the dirty boys where no job is too dirty. (718)901-2376. Yes ma'am. 4365854785697894. 11/2017. 601. Ok, thanks. You too." I listened to her one sided conversation and knew the first step in my plan had been put into motion. "It will be in tomorrow's edition," she said and handed me back the Tracfone.

"Thanks," I said and gave her the money I promised her before I walked away.

Before I got to the end of the street, I noticed three guys walking up to me. I sized each one of them up, so I'd remember them if something were to go down right now and I survived. They were all dark skinned and taller than me. One of the guys had tattoos in every area that wasn't clothed; arms, neck, and face. I couldn't tell if he had them everywhere because of his clothes, but I'm pretty sure they are. Another one of the guys had the nappiest dreads I'd ever seen with the name 'Lisa' tattooed on his neck. The last guy had seven teardrops tattooed under his right eye and a low haircut. I didn't know much about the hood but I knew from watching TV that those teardrops had several meanings. So either this man had done seven years in prison, been raped seven times in prison, killed seven people or lost seven people. Doesn't matter to me. All I know is I didn't bring a gun with me and it's three against one.

I continued to walk, ignoring their presence as they closed in on me. I could see I was close to the convenient store and my car was still there. I thought about making a run for it but I'm not fast, not to mention, bullets are faster. Plus, running makes me look suspect and since I'm not from here, everybody may draw their guns on me.

"Who you here wit?" the guy with tattoos all over his body asked me.

"Nobody," I responded as I continued to walk. I could hear them jogging up to me, so I picked up my pace. My heart began to race when I noticed he was walking alongside of me and the one with dreads was on the other side.

"You don't belong here. Why you here?" the one with the teardrops said from behind me. I turned around to face him while I backpedaled. I needed to be able to see what they were doing with their hands.

The last thing I needed was for either one of them to grab hold of me. I knew if they were to lock their arms around me, I'd be a goner. Now, I'll fight to the death of me but I know the deck is currently stacked against. I glanced back and noticed I was no longer in the projects. We were in the street in front of the convenient store. Everyone was minding their own business, unlike the people in my neighborhood, who would have called the police a long time ago.

"What do you want?" I asked as I looked at all of them in their eyes, one at a time. When I looked at the one with the teardrops, he looked away, so he would be the last one I attacked, if I needed to.

"Don't question us bitch! You da one outta place!" the one with tattoos all over said with an attitude.

"Well, I'm leaving and I was only here a little while, so let me go," I said.

"You police?" the same guy asked me.

I wanted to say, *Nigga, who would actually answer that shit honestly!* "No," I said instead.

I watched them closely as the guy with the teardrops looked at the one with nappy dreads, who then gave him a head nod. All kinds of alarms sounded off in my head! These niggas were not about to rape or kill me!

I quickly grabbed two stars and threw them at the nappy dreadhead and the one with tattoos all over his body. I grabbed my knife and charged at the third one, who had his gun drawn but his hands were shaking. He fired two bullets at me and I slid just in time, cutting both of his ankles. He fell forward onto the ground and lost his gun, and I could not believe how easy it was to take down three men. I walked closer to his head but out of his reach. "Don't kill me," he said and looked at me with teary eyes, like they weren't just about to do something to me.

"Can't leave you alive for you to come back for me later," I said before I sliced his throat.

When I stood to my feet, the smoker was standing beside me with her toothless smile, which made me queasy. "Dem boys been gang raping girls for as long as I can remember! Lemme ask you something?" she said to me with a now serious expression. I turned to face her and give her my undivided attention. "That ad. Kill?" she asked as I nodded my head. "Figured. Spreading word. What's your name?" she asked.

"Princess," I answered and turned to walk away. It took me a minute to realize she can form complete sentences when she needed to and maybe she talks so short so only the person she's talking to know what's going on.

As I approached my car, I noticed someone was sitting on my hood. I slowed my pace and noticed it was the guy I was watching shoot dice when I first got out of the car. I used my car keys to unlock the driver's side door only. My plan was to simply get a smoker to place the ad for me and go home. Not that I'm complaining about killing people but damn, it just wasn't in my plans.

"I saw what you did," he said and hopped down and walked up to me with his hands up. I just stared at him and waited on him to continue. "I'm Jeremy," he said as I nodded my head at him. He opened the car door for me while he gestured for me to get in. I didn't move because there is nothing I can do from a seated position. Noticing my hesitancy, he gave me a simple shoulder shrug.

"Princess," I said and wished I had met him under different circumstances.

"Cute. So, give me ya number and I'll have some jobs for ya," he said, which shocked the fuck out of me. Word of mouth has never traveled this damn fast!

"(718)901-2376. I can receive texts," I said and hopped in the car, locked the doors, and started the ignition, all in one swift motion. He smirked at me before he nodded his head, as I backed away from the store and headed home.

Chris Butler

It took days for a nigga to get over the bullshit with Vanessa. I've never been left unless I told the bitch to leave. Hell, I should have been the one leaving her alone, since she did the most damage! I called her like four times the day she left, like I'm the bitch. I was texting and everything. From Alexis' phone, of course, because her pickle head ass wouldn't give me the number. She even had her phone set, so the number wouldn't show up when I called her!

I knew I needed to go to the emergency room because I was still dizzy and my lip was numb. When I walked through the emergency room doors, the registration clerk smiled at me. I'll never understand these bitches. I don't come here that often but when I do, it's because I need some damn stitches and these bitches be choosing.

I walked up to the window and filled the paperwork out, so I could be seen. About thirty minutes later, I'm called to the back and the nurse asked me all types of shit. I understand she's doing her job but damn, my fucking head is killing me, my lip is split open and numb, and I haven't been able to reach Vanessa!

Once I'm in my room and shit, the same registration clerk came in to do her part and asked for money. I gave her $260 for the emergency room discount price for people without insurance. The bitch's eyes got so big when I counted the 20's out for her. Then she asked me to call her on her way out. I ain't gone lie to ya, she was bad as fuck, so I'm going to stop by on my way out and give her my number. I wrote it down on part of my receipt, so I can hand it to her on my way out.

The doctor came in and asked me the same questions the nurse already asked me. Now, I know I watched her type everything I was saying into the computer. Being as though they work at the same hospital, he should have access to those same notes so why ask me the same questions other than to see if I'm going to change it?

As many times as I've needed stitches, I should be used to that long ass numbing needle. I guess it was just something about it going through my face that had a nigga sweating. Then when the doctor was numbing the area around my mouth, his ass was poking and moving and some more shit, so it got worse before it got better. He stitched me up and told me to come back to have them removed in five to seven days. On my way out, I slid Tiffany, the clerk, the paper I had my number on and left.

Not even ten minutes later, she was texting me and told me to save her number in my phone.

I wasn't able to reach Vanessa until the next day and she pretty much told me to fuck off, so why the fuck would I chase her? I don't chase bitches. I chase money!

"You good bruh?" Phat asked me and walked in my room.

"Yea, I'm straight," I answered, not knowing why he was asking me that.

"Yo man, I know you so I got her number out of Lexis' phone," he said and laid a piece of paper with Vanessa's number on it on my nightstand.

"Naw, I'm good on that bitch dog, forreal. I'm just trying to figure out when we gone make our next move. Shit, a nigga funds getting dry," I said and knocked her number into the trash can that sat next to my nightstand.

"Shit, it's a nigga named Remy out in Newark that's been flossing. Say bruh hard to get close to though," Phat said to me.

At this point, I didn't give a fuck how hard the streets were saying it is to get close to this nigga. This nigga was about to get got! "Shit man, let me and Steve head that way so we can scope the scene out and I'll let you know what's up," I said and dapped Phatty G up.

"PHAT! Where you go?" Alexis' loud mouth ass yelled, as she looked for Phat.

I don't understand why they're always under each other. I can't do that shit. I'd get tired of seeing the same person every damn day all day. Alexis might as well move in, as much as she's here. She's here all day and she stay overnight a lot. Then when she does take her worrisome ass home, they're on the phone. She's the reason why we haven't done a hit in months. Phat always had some excuse why he can't go but I'll tell you one thing, if he back out at the last minute this time, we will still go and just split the shit four ways. It will be more money for us anyway. It ain't like he play a major role in what we do anyway.

"I'm in here talking to Chris bae!" he yelled back.

A few seconds later, she walked in the room with the biggest smile ever and when I looked over at Phat, he was smiling too. These two mufuckers are stuck on stupid! "Man, get y'all retarded asses out my damn room!" I said to them, while I shook my head.

"Fuck you, lonely ass nigga!" Phat said and laughed at me as he headed towards the door.

"You got Nessa mad at me because you used my phone to stalk her," Alexis said to me.

"Fuck Nessa," I said and leaned back on my bed.

"You wish," Alexis said and walked out of the room. I didn't even respond to that shit. I ain't on Vanessa's ass no more, fuck her, I'm doing me.

I sat around my room all day and thought about nothing. Have you ever just ain't have shit on your mind? That shit's ridiculous! I've been laying around staring at the TV because I damn sure wasn't watching it.

Tiffany: Hey boo! R U busy?

I sat up in my bed and read Tiffany's message over and over and debated on whether or not I wanted to entertain this whore. I just met the bitch yesterday and she's already calling me boo.

Chris: Naw.
Tiffany: CN I CME OVA?

Chris: yea. **4402 Robinhood Dr**

Tiffany: C ya soon

It took her about thirty minutes before she got here and was texting me saying she's outside. When I walked in the living room, Phat, Alexis, Frankie, Steve, and James were all in there watching TV. I don't know what happened between Frankie and Alexis but they haven't been arguing anymore. I'm not complaining, I'm just curious. "It's alive!" Alexis said with this horrified expression on her face, which caused us all to laugh at her silly ass!

"Man, fuck you!" I said, still laughing as I walked towards the door.

"Where you headed?" James asked me.

"Nowhere," I answered. I can't wait until I can get my own shit. Do you know how fucking annoying it is for someone to ask you where you going every time you get up? Man, I can literally be heading to the kitchen and as soon as I walk out my room, someone ask where I'm going!

I opened the door and waved Tiffany over and turned to head back to my room. "Hey everybody, I'm Tiffany," she said when she came in the living room. I looked at her crazy because ain't nobody asked her shit about herself. If I didn't take the time out to introduce you, then you ain't shit! It's just that simple. Neither Frankie nor Alexis responded to her. They were watching TV, like she hadn't just said anything. I looked over at Phat, who had given her a head nod after James and Steve spoke to her.

"You finish?" I asked her. She looked at me all confused and what not, like she ain't did shit. "Man, come one." I said, as I turned and headed to my room.

She closed the door behind her as I walked over to the couch in my room. I looked up at her and studied her movements, as I tried to figure out why she came over here. She's bowlegged so I can't tell if she want to get fuck or just got fucked, by the way she walked. She had her hair pulled back into a ponytail and if you asked me, she should have left it down. It's not long enough for a ponytail. She's wearing red low top Converse, some skinny jeans, and a red tight-fitting t-shirt. She had real small titties and not much ass but her thighs were thick as fuck. I stared at her and wondered how that happened.

"Why you go over there?" she asked me with an unreadable expression.

"Nobody is allowed in my bed but me," I stated before something on the news caught my attention. It was breaking news over in Newark. Three niggas were killed outside a convenience store and they were looking for information on the man that killed them. They didn't release any information on how they died or nothing, and nobody was talking. Hell, the store didn't even have cameras. What caught my attention is the neighborhood she said is the same neighborhood that nigga Remy hang out in. Now we're going to have to put our hit on hold until shit cooled down over there. I guess we have to pick a new target for now.

"Why not?" she asked, taking my attention away from the news.

"Just how I am. What's up?" I asked her.

"What you mean?" she asked, as she played stupid.

See, y'all bitches always trying to play stupid instead of being direct. If you go to a nigga house you just met and want to fuck him, then say that. If you just want to chill, then say that. What you don't do is show up and act like you don't know why you came over. "Why did you want to come over here?" I asked her. I watched as her smile faded and her face took on a serious expression.

"I just wanted to see you," she answered me.

"Now what?" I asked because she's wasting time that I'd never be able to get back.

"What you mean 'now what'?" she asked and I could tell she was trying not to get an attitude with me.

"You said you wanted to see me. You've seen me, so now what?" I broke it down to her.

She stood there a few seconds and looked at me like she didn't know what to say. I'm a real straightforward ass nigga and I expect the same from everybody else. Shit, if she wants to watch, a movie we can watch a movie. All she has to do is tell me. "I just want to chill with you," she said softly.

I patted the seat beside me and she walked over to the couch and sat down. "What do you want to watch?" I asked as she released a deep breath I didn't know she was holding. Her ass must have been nervous. She probably thought I was going to kick her out.

"Doesn't matter," she answered.

I turned the TV station to TNT and The Fantastic Four was on. We sat in silence and watched the movie until I started dozing off. "Are you tired?" she asked and leaned her head on my shoulder.

"Yea," I answered her.

"Let's lay down in the bed. I'm tired too," she said.

"Didn't I tell you nobody get in my bed but me?" I asked her and she didn't respond. I stood up to get a blanket out the hall closet and when I returned, she was about to climb on my bed. "Bitch, if you get in my bed, I'm gonna get my sister to knock your ass out!" I said and scared the fuck out of her.

She jumped so hard when I started talking that I thought she would fall over. "I'm not a bitch!" she said with an attitude and walked back to the couch.

"Well, quit acting like one." I said.

"Has anyone ever told you that you're an asshole?" she asked me, which caused me to think about Vanessa, since she was the last person to call me one.

"All the time," I replied and laid across my couch. She crawled on top of me and laid her head on my chest.

I pulled the blanket over us as my hands began to roam her body. I rubbed her back firmly, like I was massaging it. She tilted her head towards my face and tried to get a kiss, but I turned my head and she kissed and sucked on my neck. I grabbed her lil booty and she moaned into my neck. She shifted her body, so her pussy would be on top of my dick. As soon as I felt the heat, my dick grew! When she felt it, she started grinding on it, as she sucked on my neck. She lifted her hips, unbuckled my jeans, and freed my dick before unbuckling her own. We both wiggled out of our jeans and she stroked it with her hands. I was so into the neck sucking and hand gestures that I almost let the bitch stick my dick in her! She shifted her weight to slide me in but I pushed her off me and she fell on the floor.

"What the fuck?!" she yelled and jumped to her feet.

"Bitch, ain't no raw dogging happening over here!" I screamed back at her.

I watched as she folded her arms across her chest and began to tap her foot. It was hard looking at her face with her bare pussy sitting at eye level. "Nigga, are you gone get a condom or what?" she asked me. I didn't respond as I made my way to my nightstand. When I turned around, she was standing behind me and I almost ran her ass over. "Let's get in the bed boo," she said, barely above a whisper.

"Bitch, if you say one more thing about my damn bed, you getting the fuck out!" I screamed and walked past her back to the couch.

I was tired as fuck, so I laid back down with the cover and slid the condom on my dick. She walked back over to me and threw one leg over me, so she could straddle me. She slid down my ten-inch pipe and slowly moaned as she rotated her hips in a circular motion the whole way down. "Shit baby! You feel so good." she moaned as she rode me slowly. Her pussy was okay but it wasn't just good. Plus, she was riding my dick like she's never ridden one before. She was just going up and down real slow. Her pussy wasn't as wet as it should have been either. I grabbed her hips and guided her the way I wanted her to go and it took about five minutes, but she got it down packed. I met her halfway and grinded up into her each time as her pussy got wetter and wetter for me. She moaned my name softly and the shit turned me on and made my dick harder. I kept the same pace until she came and laid on my chest.

"Naw, don't lay down now," I told her and raised her body off mine. I got up, made her stand, and bent her over as I entered her from behind. I long stroked her as I reached around to play with her clit. A few minutes later, she was cumming again and she almost fell.

"I can't stand no more," she said and dropped down to her knees.

"You want me to stop?" I asked as she shook her head no.

"Let's get on the bed," she said and I ignored her. I was too close to nutting for her to ruin that for me. I laid her on her stomach on the couch because I didn't want her to try to kiss me as I entered her again.

'   "Play with that pussy while I fuck you, girl," I said in her ear. She reached her hand down and played with the pearl as she moaned loudly, and I pounded into her from behind. I had the couch sliding away from the wall and I kept slipping! She came one more time before I pulled out, snatched the condom off, and came all over her back.

I stood all the way up to get a towel, so I could get cleaned up enough to walk her out. After I soaped the towel up and cleaned myself off, she was still in the same spot I left her. "Wake up girl," I said as I shook her.

"Man, yo dick so good. I never came that many times before!" she said and smiled up at me.

"Thanks, let's go," I said to her.

"What? But we just..." she trailed off after I pointed to the bed.

"I told you if you brought my bed back up, you would have to leave. You didn't listen," I explained to her.

"So, you just gone treat me like ho?! Fuck me and I gotta go?" she asked with an attitude and her hands on her hips.

"Bitch, you treated yourself like a ho, so yea, go!" I said, as I lost my patience. She took a weak swing at me but I took a step back and she missed. I'd hate to have to fuck her up, so I hope she don't hit me. I turned and walked to the door, and she cursed me out the entire time she was putting her pants back on. She was still cursing when we walked through the living room that everyone was still in.

"Tiffany, ya got nut on ya shirt," Alexis said, which caused me to laugh.

Tiffany looked at me then lunged at Alexis but I caught her in the air. She started crying immediately! I've never in my entire life met a sensitive ho! I didn't try to holla at her, she initiated this shit! I didn't call her over here, she asked me if she could come over. I didn't try to fuck, she laid on top of me! I told her not to mention the bed and she did, now she has to leave!

I opened the door without saying a word as she did the walk of shame to her car. "Man, you an asshole," Phat said, as he shook his head and laughed at me.

"What I do now?" I asked confused.

"Man, we could hear everything y'all was saying in there. We been in here cracking the fuck up!" he explained.

"Especially when you were like now that you see me, what now," Alexis said as she mocked me. James never said a word or cracked a smile, he just watched TV like I wasn't standing there talking to them.

"Man whatever! That bitch knew what she came over here for. She got it, now she's gone," I said and walked back to my room to take a shower.

When I came out of the bathroom, James was sitting on the couch in my room. I gave him a head nod and started getting dressed. "Aye, I been scoping a target out man. We can move on him tonight," James said.

"Word?" I asked.

"Yea. I'm ready when y'all are," he said.

"Shit, I'm ready right now," I said as I threw on black joggers and a black t-shirt.

"Yea but Phat ain't gone leave his girl, and Steve been tripping lately," James said. I made a mental note to holla at Steve later.

"Well shit, that's more money for me, you, and Frankie," I said as his eyes lit up.

We walked into the living room to tell them we had a target we were ready to move on right now. Steve shook his head and continued watching TV. Frankie went to her room to get dressed and Phat said he wasn't feeling well. We all know that's code for Alexis ain't letting his ass go.

James stole a Jeep Cherokee for the lick we were about to hit. It wasn't until Frankie, James, and I were parked in front of a brownstone in the Bronx that I realized I hadn't asked James nothing about what was going on. "So, what's the plan?" I asked James as he shut the engine off.

"We go in through the basement doors on the side of the house where they keep everything and back out the same way. Simple," James answered me. Frankie gave me a side eye, which made me feel uneasy about the whole thing. Ignoring my gut, I shook the feeling I had off and exited the car right after James. When we got to the basement doors, I noticed Frankie hadn't gotten out of the car yet. "We don't need her in here. She can be the look out," he said with shifty eyes after he noticed my hesitancy.

I studied his movements for a few seconds and that feeling came back in my gut. "Who's the target?" I asked James.

"Huh?" he asked like I asked a trick question. Instead of responding, I turned to head back to the truck. Before I got within Frankie's view, I heard the familiar sound of a gun being cocked. The sound stopped me in my tracks as I turned face to face with a chrome 9 millimeter. "I... I... can't let you leave," James stammered as I shook my head. "I'm sorry man but Easy found out it was us that robbed his traps in Newark. He said he would let the rest of us live, if I gave him the head," James said with his head lowered. Shaking my head, I turned around to walk away. There was no way in hell I was going to walk my black ass in there to be killed.

POW

The bullet pierced my right thigh and caused me to fall over. The shit burned like a mufucker but I refused to let anyone know how bad I was hurting. Seconds later, I was airlifted by three guys and for some reason, my thoughts went to Vanessa. Because of her, I haven't been on my game. I don't understand how meeting her and spending the day with her could have my head so bad. I wish she was with me right now, instead of James' bitch ass because she's realer than he is, and I could tell by how she cut that old bitch up.

I was thrown in a chair and one guy duct taped me to it at my shoulders, across my lap, and my ankles. I looked over at James and he couldn't make eye contact with me. I still stared at him like the bitch he was for selling me out to save his own ass, not realizing that these mufuckers are probably going to kill him anyway. I sat in the chair being punched over and over in my face. My thigh was already bleeding out from James shooting me outside. "So, you like robbing niggas?" one of the guys asked me.

In return, I spat a mouthful of blood at him and looked over at James, who still wasn't looking at me. This nigga has a gun, all of their backs are to him, and instead of making shit right, he's being a coward. "The least you can do is make eye contact bitch!" I said to James before spitting more blood out my mouth.

One of the other guys hit me so hard, the damn chair fell over. "Who sent you?" he asked as he stood over me.

"Ya mama," I said and laughed until he kicked me in my stomach.

I continued to laugh because I was not about to answer no questions or beg for my life but they thought I would. "Stand this pussy back up," said the guy I assumed was their leader. The other guys sat the chair up before they took turns and hit me all over my body. "You ready to answer some questions?" the leader asked as he stared intensely at me.

"Man, I'on know where yo mama at man. I fucked her and called her a cab," I replied and matched his stare. I watched as his brown skin turned a shade darker and his temple started to throb. I knew I was pissing him off but shit, that made two of us. He hit me again and caused blood to fly out of my mouth. At this point, I really couldn't see what's going on because everything is blurry. "My bitch hit harder than you," I said and chuckled to myself at the thought of Vanessa sitting on my chest and hitting me in the face.

All of a sudden, it felt like 100 feet were kicking me over and over, all over my body. I tried to look over at James but my eyes were swollen shut. I decided to stop fighting it and just let go because the pain was just too much. I allowed my body to go limp and a few minutes later, the beating stopped.

"How many of y'all are there?" I heard a voice ask James. I laid on the ground and prayed he didn't tell them about Frankie being outside in the car. We all grew up together and I'd hate to see harm come to any of them except James.

"It's three of us. I told you I would bring the crew if you let me live," James answered with a shaky voice.

"Three of y'all took down two of my trap houses in under three hours?" the voice asked. I didn't hear a response from James, so he must have nodded his head. "Now ain't that some shit!" the voice exclaimed. "I should have had these niggas on payroll! Where the other nigga?" the voice asked.

I wanted to call out to them but I couldn't move my mouth or anything, for that matter. "She's in the truck outside," James answered.

"She?" the voice asked. "Go get her," the voice continued.

"So, y'all robbed me? You, him, and her?" the voice asked again, like he's trying to make sure. I didn't hear a response, so he must have nodded his head again.

"It wasn't my idea, it was his. He calls the shots, we just follow his lead," James rattled off and if I could move, I'd fuck him up!

"Well, he's dead so who's next in line to be the boss?" the voice asked and if I'm not mistaken, I heard a light chuckle.

"Me," a female voice that didn't belong to Frankie said.

POW POW POW

Three gunshots were the last things I heard before I let go completely and everything went dark.

Vanessa Broughton

When I got home I was so fucking excited, I didn't know what to do. I walked in and smiled, as I gave Wayne and my dad hugs. "How are my favorite guys doing this afternoon?" I asked, as I took a seat in the living room with them. My dad seemed a bit spaced out and Wayne looked perplexed by my sudden change of attitude.

"I told dad about you wanting to move out." Wayne said, getting straight to the point. It didn't even come close to dampening my spirits though.

"Good. It's not you guys. I just need to be able to spread my wings without someone questioning my every move. Here, if I walk to the bathroom too fast, someone is questioning me," I explained as I looked at my dad.

"How are you going to pay for this place?" my dad asked me.

"Well, I just got a job cleaning up, which is why I was so happy when I walked in a second ago. It pays really well," I answered him.

"How well?" my dad asked.

"Well, I'll be cleaning buildings and apartments after people are evicted. For the empty buildings, I'll be paid 2500 and for the ones people were in, its 4500. The more difficult the job, the more I charge," I said to Wayne and my dad, who both nodded their heads.

"Well, I'm happy for ya," my dad said.

"Me too," Wayne countered.

We were interrupted by the ringing of my phone. I didn't know it was the Tracfone until I grabbed my regular phone. "I'll be back guys, this my work phone," I said and exited the room. I ran to my room and grabbed a bandana to wrap around the mouth of the phone before answering. "Hello. Thanks for calling, this is Princess. How may I help you?" I answered professionally.

"Got a job for you. How dirty is too dirty?" the male voice asked.

"Nothing is too dirty for Princess. Who sent you?" I asked.

"Jeremy. I've left instructions for you on bus 91 in the third seat from the back on the left hand side, along with my phone number. Call me if you have any questions," the male voice said and I disconnected the call.

On my way out of the door, I could tell Wayne wanted to ask me where I was going but he had to know he's the reason why I want to leave. Maybe that's why he didn't ask me. Bus 91 isn't really a bus, it's an old southern style restaurant about twenty minutes away from my house. Before I parked, I circled the block a few times and checked out the scenery. Nothing looked out of place, so I hopped out and sashayed into the restaurant and took a seat at the third table on the left.

"Good evening, what can I get for you today?" the waitress asked as she approached my table.

"Um...can I get a two-piece white meat fried with mac n cheese and rice and gravy on the side? Oh and a sweet tea!" I said and smiled at her.

"I got you covered!" she said and walked away.

While she was gone, I slid my hand under the table until I felt the paper stuck to it. I peeled the paper off and discreetly stuck it in my oversized bag. A few seconds later, my phone rang. When I pulled it out and saw Alexis pop up, I almost ignored it but she was Facetiming me, so I answered. I slid my Bluetooth on my ear, so no one could hear what she was saying to me.

"Hey stranger!" she sang into the phone.

"Hey traitor," I spoke back and watched the smile disappear from her face.

"Listen, I didn't know you didn't want to talk to him. I thought you just hadn't given him your number yet," she explained.

"It's cool, what you doing?" I asked her.

"Chilling with Phat. Where are you?" she asked.

"Bus 91," I answered.

"Ooooh, somebody trying to get some meat on them bones eating there! Girl, you know them cooks straight outta Mississippi!" she said all country like, which caused me to laugh. I was so glad I had the Bluetooth in because they probably would have gotten offended and spit in my food or something. "Nessy, on a date baby, look," Alexis said and turned the phone so Phat could see me.

"No, I'm not," I said and smiled.

"Well, who is that behind you?" she questioned, which caused me to look over my shoulder.

"Can I join you?" he asked.

"Um… sure," I answered him. "Hey Lex! I'll call you later, k?"

"Ok. Don't be cheating on Chris," she said with a wink.

I hung the phone up before I tossed it in my bag and removed my Bluetooth. "So, to what do I owe this pleasure?" I asked and shocked myself with my boldness.

"Well, you are a beautiful woman and I can tell you about your business. I haven't been able to get you off my mind, since I saw what you could do. I've sent so much business your way, so you will be extremely busy the next couple of days. Now, after that, will you allow me to take you out?" he asked as I smiled bashfully.

"What was your name again?" I asked playing dumb because I knew who he was from the moment I looked up in his face.

"Jeremy," he said and smirked at me, like he knew I knew who he was.

"Well Jeremy, that will be fine with me," I said as my Tracfone started to ring. I signaled to Jeremy to give me one moment while I took the call.

"Hello. This is Princess, how may I help you?" I answered the phone.

"Did you get the package?" the voice asked.

"Yes, I'll review it after dinner and get to it first thing in the morning," I said and he hung up the phone. When I made it back to my table, my food was there and Jeremy was just about to eat off my plate when I smacked the fuck out of his hand. He yelped out before shaking his hand and looking at me crazy.

"Girl, what the fuck you hit my hand with?" he asked and made me realize that I smacked his hand with this thick ass

Tracfone. I held it up to show him before I shrugged and sat down.

"I don't share my food. Order your own," I said before I bowed my head to say my grace.

When I looked back up, Jeremy was looking at me sideways. "What?" I asked, as I dug into my food.

"You pray?" he asked, like he didn't just see me say my grace.

"All the time. You don't?" I asked, confused about why my praying shocked him.

"You killed three men in like fifteen seconds though, man," he said and whispered so low that I had to lean closer to him to hear.

"What does that have to do with my relationship with God?" I asked him seriously. I wasn't understanding what he was getting at by bringing old shit up. He didn't respond, he just shook his head. I guess I wouldn't be hearing from him to take me out after all. And to think, it's all because I said grace over my food. After I finished eating, I told Jeremy I had to go and he understood, with no questions asked.

When I made it home, I went straight to my room to read over the instructions I was given. This woman had a routine that she followed strategically, which is good when nobody's trying to kill you! She's beautiful, light skinned with long brown hair with blonde highlights. I noticed she had a kid that's four because her bedtime is at 8:30. He didn't list what he'd like me to do with the child, so I'd just have to wing it. Now I'm going to charge him 6000 dollars, for the inconvenience of this kid.

I grabbed my phone to call him up and he answered on the first ring. "$6000," I said into the phone. He didn't respond right away but he agreed. "I can clean up tonight if you can pay tonight," I said to him, eager to make six bands. He agreed, I gave him my account information, and once I checked the balance, I saw he had transferred the money into my account!

I was beyond excited as I got dressed! The only thing specific he wanted done was her hands delivered to an address not far from her house. I grabbed five throwing stars, a knife that could cut through bone, and my Ashiko boots. To top my weaponry off, I put my gripping gloves on. Finally, I was dressed in all black and headed to my car.

It wasn't long before I pulled up to a beautiful brownstone. I checked the time and it was 8:30. When I looked back up at the window, the light had just been cut off. Right on schedule!

I moved my car to the next road over and parallel parked it before I got out and cut through a yard to get to my target's house. I walked to the back door and realized the sliding door was unlocked as I slid my way in and into the pantry. Seconds later, she walked in the kitchen straight to the sliding door and locked it. I held my breath as she walked around the kitchen and wiped everything off. I knew I could take her but it'd be less noise if I surprised her. Plus, I didn't want the kid to wake up and come down here.

Almost ten minutes later, she was done cleaning the kitchen, and I followed her into the living room and made sure to stay in the shadows. She plopped down on the couch and turned the tv on. I crept up behind her, grabbed her ponytail and yanked it back to give me more access to the neck. I used my left hand to slice her from her right ear to her left ear, so when the police came, they would think it was a lefty that did it. I then moved around the couch and chopped her hands off.

I kept my hood pulled tightly around my face as I walked around and looked for a cordless phone. I came up short but almost stepped in a puddle and the piss was so strong. I opened the door to the little girl's room and saw the glow from the phone in the closet. I could hear her saying a man killed her mommy as I closed the room door back. I was looking for a phone to call 911 but since she had already done that, my job was done.

I left the same way I came, hopped in my car, and headed to the house not far from here. I checked the address, did a light jog up the driveway, and made her hands stick the middle finger up before sitting them on the porch. Afterwards, I headed home. As I walked through the door, I sighed heavily because Wayne was up waiting on me. "Not now Wayne. That house was filthy and I need to shower," I said as he nodded his head. I hopped in the shower and went to bed.

The next morning, my Tracfone was ringing off the hook. "Hello," I answered.

"Bus 91. Same table. I got you a new job," the all too familiar voice of Jeremy said on the other end. I guess today I'd be eating breakfast there.

"Hey Sweetie!" Alexis sang into the phone after she answered.

"Girl, I'm starving I'm about to get some breakfast from Bus 91," I said.

"I wish I could join you but James and Chris trying to get Phat to hit a lick with them, and it's so dangerous. I'm not leaving until they leave," she said with a laugh. I laughed with her because she had Phat wrapped her around her finger. When I pulled up to the restaurant, I shut the engine off and ended my call.

I made my way to my table with my oversized purse and felt under the table for my instructions. I wasn't really hungry, so I ordered an omelet, ate it, and left.

When I got home, I ran straight to my room so I could read the instructions. I opened them and there were three pictures and an address. There was a note telling me to go in through the front door because they only used the basement door. I knew this was a job that had to happen at night time. I laid around my room and listened to music as I tried desperately to become one with myself, so I would be focused tonight.

As the hours passed me by, it felt like days. Finally, it was time for me to make more money. I checked my bank account online and noticed $8000 had been transferred, so he must have given me a $500 bonus.

I pulled up and checked the scenery before I drove to the next street over. I hopped out my car to hop over an extra tall ass fence. I had to jump on their trash can to get over it. I walked around to the front of the brownstone and placed my ear to the door. It was thick as fuck and I couldn't really hear shit, so I decided to take my chances and just walk in.

Surprisingly, no one was in the foyer or the living room. "He bringing the whole crew here?" I heard a voice ask.

"Hell yeah and I'm killing all them niggas," another voice responded. I tiptoed passed the room they were in, as I looked for the basement door. When I found it, it squeaked so I made a mad dash down the steps before I hid in the shadows. They had one light bulb that was swinging in the middle of the basement. I sat on the floor Indian-style, so my legs wouldn't get tired.

About fifteen minutes later, I heard a single gunshot before feet trampled down the stairs. I watched three guys run out the basement side door and come back in holding a man that was bleeding. I recognized the other guy but I couldn't put my finger on where I saw him. I watched them beat the guy in the chair until he wasn't moving. The guy was either really strong or really dumb because he was talking crazy every time they asked him a question. It didn't take me long to figure out that the guy standing had set the other guy up. After that, the guy standing said it was a girl outside that also helped them rob the trap houses.

Now, I'm no rocket scientist but Alexis had told me about Phat nem robbing people but I think it's five of them. Oh shit! It's a good thing Alexis didn't let Phat leave or he will be dead just like, oh shit! Nooo, Chris! That meant Frankie was outside! I can't even go warn her! Fuck! I watched as the other men ran out the door to get Frankie. I heard three shots and I hoped it was Frankie shooting and that she connected. I already knew that these three guys were the guys on my hit list, so it didn't matter at this point who did the killing. "Who's the boss now that he's dead?" the leader said.

"Me," I answered him.

His ass had no clue where I was and just started shooting. I grabbed a throwing star and threw it I hit the traitor in the neck and dropped him instantly. I grabbed two more and hit the leader in both eyes, as he screamed like a bitch while he fired like crazy. He fell over and I raised from my seated position and retrieved my knife. I walked over to him slowly and stabbed him three times in the neck and killed him. I heard gurgling noises and walked over to the traitor. He was pleading with me with shocked filled eyes as I slit his throat. I walked over to Chris and right before I was going to walk away, I noticed his chest rising and falling. I ran upstairs and put water in a pot, came back down, and dumped it on his face. He woke up groaning. I wiped the blood off my knife, so I could cut him loose. When he fell out of the chair, he groaned some more.

"Chris, I can't carry your big ass outta here, you gone have to walk," I said as I stared at his badly bruised face.

"Nessa?" he asked, probably because he couldn't see me.

"Yea. Long story. I'll tell ya later but right now, we gotta get outta here," I answered him.

I helped him stand and we walked over to the stairs but he stopped. "Frankie," he said with his head hung low.

"I don't know," I answered and he rotated to turn to go out the other way. He has got to be the dumbest nigga ever! I must be even dumber because I helped him get out the basement side door.

Frankie was holding them off pretty good and I threw stars at the three I saw. "What you doing here?" Frankie asked, once we were close enough for her to see my face.

"Long story. Let's take my car," I responded to her. Frankie and I kicked the fence down, so Chris didn't have to climb it to make it to the car. I unlocked the doors then heard the familiar sound of a gun being cocked. Fuck!

Steve

It was taking James longer than expected to pull this shit off. Ok, I know you're thinking we all grew up together like family but that's bullshit! Phatty G and Chris always got every bitch they wanted! They were sharing bitches but never tried to pass anyone off to me or James! When I turned eighteen and was able to leave the group home we were in, I was the one who found an apartment for us to live in. So, can someone please tell me how the fuck I ended up sleeping on the couch? I know it was Phat's idea because his ass can persuade the beach to buy sand. It's my apartment but I'm the one sleeping from couch to couch. They have always treated James and I like the stepchildren. It's a three-bedroom apartment and Frankie, Chris, and Phat each have their own rooms. Frankie would have had her own regardless because she's the only female but what I don't like about her is she's ride or die for Chris and Phat, but not me and James. She wasn't even supposed to be included tonight but she tagged along because Chris came.

Ever since Vanessa came over, shut me down and stayed the night with Chris, I've been plotting against them. That same night I drove over to where I knew a few of Easy E's workers hung out at this bar. I sat at the bar and sipped on water and pretended it was fucking me up, and I mentioned how James and his crew had robbed some trap houses not far from there. When one of the guys asked me what I said, it simply set the plan in motion. I knew they would find James and he would tell to save his own ass. I also knew that after they killed everybody, they would kill James too and nothing would be traced back to me.

As I sat outside parked a few houses down watching, I noticed a slim person walk in through the front door. I couldn't tell whether or not they were male or female. I guess they brought in backup just in case Chris got the upper hand. Not long after that, a jeep pulled up and out hopped Chris and James. I could see Frankie seated in the jeep and it had me wondering what happened, since we all normally get out for the heist. Not long after that, I saw that Chris didn't want to go in and hit the lick. I don't know what happened that spooked him but he turned and walked away and headed back to the jeep. James surprised the fuck out of me when he shot him in the leg. I'm glad he was smart enough not to kill him because Easy wants the head. A few seconds later, three of Easy's goons came outside and carried Chris inside through the basement doors.

I'd give anything to be able to see what's going on inside right now. Too bad I have no way to get in and out undetected. They were inside so long, I lost track of time and began to doze off when two guys came outside and headed towards the jeep. Frankie, being alert as always, saw them coming because she had done slid out the back door, and I didn't see her until she was firing at them.

She knocked them both off too, which shocked me because I didn't know she was a good shot. Frankie has always hated guns, although she's never told us why, so to see how good she is with her guns made me wonder how she got so good with a weapon she hates. Three other guys came out of nowhere and she wasn't in the position to knock them off, so she was shooting recklessly and wasting ammunition. They were closing in on her and my dick was getting hard because I was so excited! All of a sudden, they dropped like flies! I looked over and saw the slim cat walking out while helping someone out. I zoomed in on them the closer they walked through the backyard and saw it was Chris!

I began to panic immediately because I don't know if James knew I set him up and if he did know, then I don't know if he told them. As I watch them kick down the fence, I realized they must have parked on the other side. I quickly cranked my car up, well my borrowed car, and sped over to the street and blocked in the silver Impala. I hopped out and walked right up on them as the slim guy unlocked the doors.

They were so focused on getting Chris in the car safely that no one was paying attention until I cocked my hammer. It wasn't until the slim guy said "Fuck!" that I realized it wasn't a guy at all.

"Take your fuckin hood off before I blow ya fuckin face off bitch!" I said to her, so I could see who she was.

"Fuck you pussy!" she said to me, which caused me to clench my jaws. "Take it off me ya damn self, fuckin traitor!"

she said, like she knew who I was. Well, she obviously knew us because she's with Frankie and Chris but how?

I took a step closer and Chris fainted. I guess because of all the pain he was in. Frankie grabbed him before he hit the ground but it made her lose her balance and he fell on top of her. The other bitch didn't flinch or try to help because her eyes were trained on me. It's something familiar about her but I can't place it.

Taking another step closer to her, I noticed she got in a fighting stance. This bitch really thought she could whoop me! It was almost comical! "Who the fuck are you?" I asked her with clenched teeth, getting pissed off at the audacity of this bitch!

"Come closer so I can show you?" she said seductively, which caught me off guard. I smiled a little bit and took another step closer to her when she crouched down low and spin kicked me. I hit the ground so hard, I couldn't catch my breath.

The bitch didn't give me time to either. She jumped on my chest and punched me over and over in my face. I was starting to lose consciousness and I couldn't feel the gun in my hand anymore, so I must have dropped it when I fell. Not long after her attack started, everything went black.

Vanessa

Hearing the gun cock when we were so close to the car had me wishing we had just gotten into the jeep they stole to come over and switch cars. The only reason I didn't want to get in the jeep was because it was stolen and I didn't want my name tied to anything, considering my current line of work. When we came face to face with another one of their friends, my blood began to boil! How can you grow up with someone you're not related to but they treat you like family and turn on them like this?

"Take your fuckin hood off before I blow ya fuckin face off bitch!" he said to me. I knew I couldn't allow him to see who I was because if we didn't kill him tonight, he would eventually put everything together and realize Princess and I are one in the same. I don't want anyone knowing about Princess, except those I trust but looking at Chris' situation, I think I'm going to keep it to myself. I know I'm going to have to come up with some type of explanation about my reason for being here and being able to help them in their time of need.

"Fuck you pussy!" I said and glared at him. "Take it off me ya damn self, you fuckin traitor!" I said as I still stared at him with my hood pulled tightly over my face. I was so busy studying his movements that when Chris passed out and fell on top of Frankie, I didn't have time to react to it. Hopefully Frankie is fine because I cannot put both of them in my car. Hell, I can't even put Chris in my car alone.

"Who the fuck are you?" he said through clenched teeth, like he was scaring some damn body. I wanted to attack him straight up but I couldn't afford to get throwed off my game with no back up. Frankie hadn't even attempted to get Chris off of her so she could stand back up, so I knew it was up to me to get us out of here. Thinking smart, I decided to take a different approach. I'm not exactly your ordinary seductress but I watch a lot of movies.

"Come closer, so I can show you?" I said with the most seduction I could muster up. I couldn't believe it worked, but I watched as his body relaxed and he took another step closer.

I stared at him a few seconds to see how relaxed he really was and as hard as it is to believe, this nigga let his guard completely down. I dropped low doing a low spinning sweep kick. His legs came from under him and he was on the ground trying to catch his breath. In a matter of seconds, I slipped my brass knuckles on and was on him like there was no tomorrow.

I punched him over and over until his head went limp. "C'mon V. We gotta go before the cops show up," Frankie said as I was grabbing my knife out. I could hear sirens in the distance and knew she was right. I stood to my feet before I rolled Chris off her. I stared at his badly beaten and bruised face and felt so bad for him.

"Help me stand him up," I said to Frankie and grabbed one arm as she followed suit and grabbed the other.

"On 3. 1. 2. 3," I said as we pulled him to a seated position. He's heavier than he looked and the fact that he can't help us is making it harder. "Go open the back door. We're going to have to pull him until we get him to the door," I said to Frankie. I waited for her to come back and we both grabbed his arms and drug his body to the back car door. "Get in and pull while I lift," I said to Frankie as she nodded her head before she crawled in the back seat of my car. It took us what seemed like forever to get his extra heavy ass in the back seat.

We finished right on time though because the police had just pulled up at the house that everything took place. I quickly but quietly shut the door before I hopped in the driver's seat, cranked the car up, and drove away. "Vanessa, will you please pull over? I can't feel my legs. Let me get up front with you," Frankie said from the back seat. Without responding, I pulled over to the shoulder of the road and popped the trunk. Frankie's eyes got as big and as round as saucers, like I was about to do something to her. It made me wonder how she was able to tag along to rob people with them all these years.

"What you looking stupid for? Get out and get in the front," I said to her and she released a big breath, which caused me to chuckle to myself. I walked to my trunk, got a blanket out and covered Chris with it, and hopped back in the car. When I saw Wendy's, I pulled off the highway to get me a bite to eat.

"What are you doing?" Frankie asked me.

"What the fuck do people normally do at Wendy's?" I asked her as I pulled up to the drive thru speaker.

I ordered a Jr bacon cheeseburger and ten-piece nugget for myself and two chicken sandwiches for Chris. "How can you eat at a time like this?" Frankie asked after I finished ordering.

"A time like what, Frankie? A time y'all almost got killed but were saved, only to almost get killed again but to be saved again?" I asked, getting aggravated. She was pissing me off because instead of thanking me, she was questioning me like I didn't have the right to eat! Shit, I'm gone always eat! We went and got something to eat after chopping Ms. Jackson up and feeding her to the pigs, so I'm most definitely going to eat after surviving a situation like the one we just survived. She didn't respond to me.

After I got my food, we went on to their apartment. I walked to the door to get Phat and take my food in the house. "What you doing here?" he asked.

I ignored him as I stepped around him to put my food in the kitchen. When I walked back out, Alexis was standing there with him, just as surprised as he was. "Long story. Chris got hurt real bad. He's passed out in my car and I need your help getting him out," I said to Phat. He didn't ask any questions, hell, he didn't even put shoes on. He just walked out the house.

Alexis and I followed behind him and when Frankie saw everyone coming, she hopped out the car. "How y'all end up together?" Alexis whispered to me.

"Long story," I said to her before I opened the back door.

"What the fuck man!" Phat yelled as soon as he saw Chris. He grabbed him up like he weighed nothing and carried him inside with tears in his eyes. We walked in just as Phat was slamming Chris' bedroom door.

I was ready to eat and Alexis looked like she had 101 questions that weren't about to get answered tonight. I grabbed my food out the kitchen and headed to Chris' room. When I opened the door, Phat shot me an evil glare that I ignored as I sat my food on the nightstand. Grabbing my gift and opening it, I set everything up on my bedside table to eat. When I looked at Phat, he was shaking his head at me. I just shrugged my shoulders as I turned the TV on Pretty Little Liars.

"What happened?" Phat asked me after he calmed down. I noticed he waited until I finished my food too. I guess Alexis has just been telling everybody about my connection with food, and I didn't mind one bit.

"Well..." I started but stopped because I was trying to figure out if I could trust him. I turned towards him and stared at him for a few seconds. After thinking about his reaction when he found Chris, I knew I could trust him. Alexis has always been there for me, so I knew I could trust her. Frankie seemed to be down for Phat and Chris, so in order to say this once, I would to tell them all at once. For some reason, I didn't want to leave Chris' side until he was awake.

"Call Alexis and Frankie in here," I said to him. He stood up and walked over to the door and called their names. When they walked in, I suddenly remembered that I didn't kill Steve and he had a key. I hopped up and ran into the living room. I locked the deadbolt and the door knob lock before getting a chair from the kitchen table. I put the back of the chair under the door knob so even with his key, he wouldn't be able to get in without alarming someone.

When I turned back around, Alexis and Phat were standing in the hall staring at me like I was crazy. "You'll understand in a minute," I said and walked past them back into Chris' room. "Ok, I trust that this won't leave this room," I said as I looked everybody in the face before continuing. I waited for each of them to give me a head nod.

DING My phone chimed and halted me again. I signaled them to give me one moment while I checked the message. I almost ignored it because it came from my regular phone, but I knew anything could be happening.

79560: checking out new balance: $24,500. To stop automatic balance updates reply S

"What's wrong?" Alexis asked, which caused me to look up from my phone.

"Close ya damn mouth," Phat said, causing me to place my hand over it like I was making sure it was still open. Once I gathered my thoughts of this large sum of money that I just found out I had, I knew my work phone would be ringing shortly.

"So, I have to start from the beginning, so you guys will understand everything. Now, hopefully y'all can fill in my blanks afterwards because I'm a little bit confused too," I said as I looked at all of them. I watched as Frankie and Phatty G exchanged glances as they did a brief head nod. "Ok. So, I wanted to move out of my house-" I began but was cut off by Phat sighing heavily.

"Why do you want to move out?" Alexis asked and caused me to roll my eyes.

"Because I'm 24 and I'm tired of them asking me where I'm going whenever I walk out of the door," I answered her.

"Well, where are you going to live and how will you pay for it with no job?" she asked with a concerned expression. See I know everybody treat me the way they do because they care, but the shit is so aggravating! I just want to live alone, walk around naked if I want to, and come and go as I please.

"If you would let me finish, you won't have any questions," I snapped at her. Right when she was about to say something back, Phat snapped his fingers really loud in her face and silenced her before she could get a word out.

"Go ahead," he said to me before he looked at Chris. I followed his glance and felt sorry for him in his current state.

"Ok, so I don't really have job related skills. The only thing I know that I've mastered is the art of killing. I decided I'd become a hit man or hit woman, whatever, doesn't fucking matter-"

"Wait, what?!Are you fucking crazy Nessa?! Do you want to go to jail?!" Alexis screamed and cut me off. I looked over at Phat to see if he was going to snap his finger or something, but he just looked at me.

"Can I finish?" I asked as I tried to remain calm. Alexis and I hardly ever got into fights and we've never been in a fist fight, and I don't want to come to blows with her because I will hurt her. She crossed her arms over her chest before she rolled her eyes inward and sighed. "Anyway, I decided to place an ad in the newspaper but I knew I couldn't do it myself, so I drove over to Newark." I noticed when I said Newark, Phat's eyes got big and he and Frankie shared another glance.

"I don't remember the name of the projects but I ran into this smoker named Kim and I paid her to make the call to place the ad. On my way out, there were three dudes trying to do something to me. I ain't know what was up until I killed them. Them niggas had been gang raping bitches!" I said to them.

"That was you?" Phat asked as I nodded my head.

"That shit was all over the news Yo!" Frankie said and spoke up for the first time since we started talking. Alexis beamed like a proud parent, once again. She swear she doesn't agree with what I enjoy doing but whenever I do it good, she be all proud and shit like she taught me everything I know.

"Anyway, when I got to my car there was this guy sitting on it. We chatted about my business briefly and he said he would be sending business my way. Tonight was my second job. I have no idea who hired me, all I know is I was supposed to kill three guys," I explained and paused briefly because I thought I heard Chris make a noise. I stopped and stared at him for a few seconds but he didn't make another sound, so I figured I was tripping.

"So, I had the address to this brownstone. I crept in through the front door and hid in the basement. I'm crouched down when I hear a gunshot and then the three guys I've been hired to kill run through the basement and out the door. When they came back in, they were carrying Chris and James walked in behind him," I said as Frankie's eyes started to water. Phat followed my eyes and looked at Frankie as well. When he made a move to get up, probably to console her, Alexis shot him a look which caused him to sigh and sit back.

"I wanted to help so bad but had I revealed my position, we would all be dead," I said and shook my head.

"How'd you get the drop on dem fools b?" Phat asked me.

"James told one of the guys Frankie was outside and she helped him and Chris rob some trap houses. When they walked out, I caught the leader and James by surprise. I killed them both then tried to help Chris out the way I came in, but he wanted to help Frankie," I said and looked over at her. She couldn't hold the tears back anymore. I watched as they fell freely from her eyes as she cried silently and held herself while she rocked. Both Alexis and Phat shook their heads at the story as they waited for me to continue.

"I helped Frankie take down the men gunning for her outside and we tried to get Chris to my car but that other guy that live here pulled a gun out on us. I tried to kill him but I don't think I did," I said and lowered my head in defeat.

"How the fuck you try and kill him but you don't think you did, yet you killed all them other mufuckers?" Phatty G asked with an attitude.

"Chill out Phat! I stopped her. The police were pulling up and we still had to get Chris in the car," Frankie explained. Phat rotated his body, so he'd be looking directly at Chris. I watched his body tense up as he clenched his jaws together. All of a sudden he stood up and stormed out the room. We heard a loud crash then the door slammed.

Phatty G

Man, I'm pissed off listening to that bullshit man, forreal. Man, we the only family we fucking got and them niggas turned snake and for what? That's the only question I got! Why the fuck did you do it, bruh? After all the bullshit we went through together, it came down to this. I'll never understand how a person you've done nothing but ride for will turn their back on you like you're nothing!

Because of James and Steve's bitch made asses, Chris is laid up in the bed passed the fuck out. I couldn't sit there and look at him with his face swollen and cut the fuck up like that. Shit, I even got mad at Vanessa because she didn't kill Steve too. Now I'm glad she didn't because I'm going to ask him why before I put a hot one between his eyes. I wish I was there but at the same time, I'm glad Alexis give me such a hard time about these streets because shit could have gone a lot worse.

Looking at my brother had me ready to fuck some shit up. I hopped up and left after I threw the chair Vanessa put behind the door against the wall. I didn't even care that it broke upon impact, I just kept on going. I left walking and it's fucked up that I have to walk because I don't know how to steal a car. Shit, I need to link up with Vanessa's ass and get this money with her. Shit, I know she about to be making a killing just by knocking mufuckers off. I don't know why I never thought about that. I'd have to keep it away from Alexis though because I know if she was always riding me about robbing niggas, she's really going to be on my case about killing them.

I've had to listen to her vent about having a best friend that enjoys the kill our whole damn relationship. She just recently started to embrace Vanessa the way she was by allowing her to do her. I was so shocked when Alexis came to me and asked if we could abduct that old lady for Vanessa's birthday. It was quite comical really. It was like we gave her a person for her birthday and from what I heard from Chris, she enjoyed the shit. We should have had her on our team, instead of James and Steve.

I walked into a convenience store and the Asian female clerk stared at me instantly. I walked to the back to grab a beer and I saw she had come from behind the counter. She was short but I can sense her presence near me and it pissed me off. "What bitch? You wanna take a swig?" I asked her and gestured towards the beer as I opened it.

"You open, you buy!" she said to me.

"Bitch, if I didn't plan on buying it, I wouldn't have opened it!" I yelled and headed towards the counter. When I looked back at her, she was behind me. "How the fuck you gone ring the shit up from back here?" I asked her, getting pissed off. She looked passed me, so I turned around and she was standing in front of me. Well, another Asian lady that looked just like her was standing there, which caused me to do a double take. I slammed a twenty-dollar bill on the counter and walked out of the store without waiting for my change. Shit, I went in there to get a beer so I could cool off and ended up even more mad. This was just something else to add to it.

I pulled my phone out of my pocket and noticed that Alexis hadn't called so she must still be chatting it up with Vanessa about the shit that's going on. I needed to clear my mind though, so I decided to do the only thing left to do.

"Long time no hear," she said as she answered the phone.

"Where you at?" I asked her.

"Around the corner from you. Want me to come through?" she asked me.

"Naw, I'm out walking around trying to clear my head. I'll be over there in a few," I said and disconnected the call. It took me about fifteen minutes to walk to the apartments she hung out at around the corner from me. Had I had condoms on me, it wouldn't have taken that long but I had to stop at another store to get some.

When I walked up her and her girls, Alisha and Stephanie, were sitting outside. They were all giving me the "come fuck me" look but I didn't have long enough to fuck them all. "Come on," I said to her and walked passed them and headed into the building. We walked up the stairs into Alisha's apartment and she wasted no time unbuckling my jeans and snatching them around my ankles. She took my whole dick into her mouth and deep throated me every time. I don't even think she came up for air. She kept making these gagging noises that were turning me the fuck on because Alexis doesn't ever take me all the way in. Alexis will suck the head and stroke the rest of it but Brittany is the fucking truth! That's why me and Chris been fucking her all these years. I'm sure she thinks one day someone will wife her but it will never be me. After she drained my man, she stood to her feet and grabbed my hand to escort me to the back room.

"Bitch, I am not getting on that bed!" I snapped at her when I noticed she was leading me to a bed I'm sure she fucks everybody on.

"What's with y'all and fucking in beds?" she asked curiously about Chris and I. See, I have no problem fucking in a bed. Alexis and I do it in the bed a lot, well if we make it to it. As for Chris, I know he just doesn't like fucking where he sleeps and I think that's because he doesn't like washing. He still makes Frankie wash his dirty laundry.

"We talking or fucking?" I asked her, getting aggravated. She looked around the room like she was trying to figure out where we would get down at. "Shit, the floor is better than the bed," I said to her. I hadn't fucked on the floor in a while because Alexis doesn't like to be on the floor.

I watched as Brittany took her clothes off and laid on the floor. I followed suit and made sure my phone was locked and wouldn't dial out. Grabbing a condom out of my pocket, I rolled it down my dick as I approached her with her legs wide open. She looked good enough to eat but I knew better. Hell, if it wasn't for that pussy tightening cream she use, she wouldn't even be fuckable. I got down on my knees and slid into her tight walls, slowly at first. She moaned loudly as she adjusted to my size. It felt so good being inside of her that I had to close my eyes.

I'm normally able to control myself but she felt so different. She was getting wetter and wetter by the second. I gave her long, slow, deep strokes while I grinded into her. Shit was feeling so good. I didn't want to stop but I couldn't help it. I could feel my dick twitching which indicated I was about to cum. I rode the wave all the way out and collapsed on top of her. "That was so good," she said from under me. I rolled off her and couldn't believe my eyes when I looked down. The condom was broken and I realized I just came all in this bitch!

Chris

As I lay in my bed in so much pain, all I can do is thank God for Vanessa. I have never thanked God for nothing in my life but he sent Vanessa in my life for a reason. From the moment I saw her, I wanted her in a different way. I know she wants me too but I already know she's going to run from it because of the fight we had. If she didn't care about a nigga, I'd be dead. She wouldn't have intervened at all. I wasn't completely out of it, well at least not all the time so I heard bits and pieces of what's going on and why she was there to begin with.

I remember her stopping to get food and I was thinking that same thing as Frankie until Vanessa said why she was getting something to eat. Maybe if I would have died, she wouldn't have stopped to get food. I'm just glad she didn't take me to the hospital. I have no idea how I got in my bed or why all these mufuckers chose to talk in my room. I could smell food and I knew only Vanessa was bold enough to eat in my bed. When I get up, if they're any crumbs in my bed, that's her ass! I heard Vanessa saying she killed those guys in Newark that I saw on the news the day I fucked Tiffany. I tried talking to them, so they would know I was up shortly after that, but my voice was muffled. Trying to speak hurt so bad that I passed out again.

When I woke up, everybody was gone except for Vanessa. I tried opening my eyes but I couldn't because they were so heavy. I started moving my arm but it hurt so freaking bad, I just gave up. I felt movement from Vanessa, leading me to believe I woke her up. "If you're awake, squeeze my hand," she said before she placed her small hands in mine. I gave it the strongest squeeze I could and I could hear her chuckle lightly. I tried speaking again but the pain stopped me. I felt the weight being removed from my eyes and I was able to see out of one of them. "The swelling went all the way down in one eye but I need to put the ice bag back on the other one," she said before she sat the ice back on my face. I just felt better knowing I could see.

"Phat stormed out a few hours ago and he hasn't made it back yet. Want me to tell Alexis you're awake, so she can call him?" she asked me. I just stared at her in pure admiration. I couldn't speak so I just stared at her until she realized why I hadn't responded. "Squeeze once for no and twice for yes," she said and giggled. I'm glad she found the humor in this shit because I didn't see a damn thing funny. I squeezed her hand twice. When she got ready to slide her hand out of mine, I gripped it again. We stared at each other for several seconds. "You're welcome," she said and bent down to kiss my cheek before she hopped out of my bed and ran out the room.

A few minutes later, Alexis and Frankie came running back in the room. Alexis was smiling with the phone to her ear while Frankie was crying. I haven't seen Frankie in years, so I just stared at her. She walked over to me slowly. "Can I hug him?" she asked Vanessa, who laughed in response.

"Why you asking me?" Vanessa asked, still laughing.

"Probably because yo ass been playing guard dog all damn night!" Alexis said while she laughed. I glanced over at Vanessa, who was turning red. Frankie walked slowly to me and gave me a one arm hug.

"Yea. If he can talk, he hasn't said anything. Ok. Where you been? Ok." Alexis said into the phone. "He's on his way." she said with a half-smile.

"Can I talk to you real quick Lex?" Vanessa asked her. Alexis didn't respond, she just got up and headed out of the room. Vanessa walked up to the door and stopped just before leaving completely out of my room. "Don't leave him alone," she said to Frankie before she followed Alexis.

Frankie turned to me with her eyes watering up. "I'm sorry Chris. I should have known something wasn't right. I wasn't feeling it and I should have said something. I'm glad your hitta came when she did! She's trying to pretend like she doesn't like you but we can tell she do. I can tell you like her too," Frankie said to me. I closed my eyes like I was going to sleep because I didn't want to try to talk about it. I was still hurting and she wanted to talk about somebody liking somebody else. The only thing I'm trying to think about is getting better and getting out of this damn bed. I got two people I need to kill, James and Steve, and the only way that will happen is if I get better and get out of this bed.

Attempting to fight through the pain, I used my arms to pull myself up into a seated position. I moaned and groaned the entire time. Frankie made a move to help me but I shot her a look and she sat back down. I swung my legs over the side of the bed one at a time. I could feel the sweat pouring down my face from the amount of pain I was in. I stood up and felt lightheaded but I needed to push through that too. I took a few steps before I fell over and landed on top of Vanessa.

"What the hell you doing out of bed boy?!" she asked from underneath me. I groaned in pain but didn't make a move to get off her. She smelled so good and the fact that my dick was pressed against her wasn't helping. "You may not be able to stand up right now but I can feel someone who can." she said and laughed, which caused me to chuckle a little bit. It hurt like hell but this girl is something else.

"Y'all so damn nasty!" Frankie said as she walked out of the room.

A few minutes later, Phat walked in the room and laughed, which caused me to look up with my one good eye. "What the hell y'all doing man?" he asked while he laughed because I was still laying on top of her. She had been making noises like she couldn't breathe trying to give me a hint, but I ignored them.

"Get him off please," she said like she was dying. I rolled off her and onto the floor hitting my back harder than I would have liked to.

"Man, I know yo ass can't walk and you trying to fuck?" Phat asked me as he shook his head.

"Fuck…. you." I got out and caused him to laugh.

"He ain't the only one trying to fuck," Vanessa said, causing us both to look at her. She was grilling the fuck out of Phat and I had no idea why.

Vanessa

I couldn't believe my fucking nose when Phat squatted down to help Chris up. He smelled just like his room smelled the day I watched him and Alexis getting it in. Knowing that he wasn't smelling like this before he left let me know what he's been out doing. I tried so hard to bite my tongue but I literally just calmed Alexis down because of a feeling she had! I just told my best friend not to get upset over an assumption but she was right! She told me that she called him three times before he answered the phone. So, he couldn't answer because he was out doing something with someone else that he could have been in his room doing with her!

"Man, I know yo ass can't walk and you trying to fuck?" Phat asked Chris as he shook his head.

I damn near gave myself whiplash, I whipped my neck in their direction so hard! "Fuck…. You," Chris croaked out. I guess he'll be talking without pain pretty soon. Phat laughed at him like he ain't sitting here smelling like sex!

"He ain't the only one trying to fuck," I said and both of them looked at me. "You know you have some nerve storming out of here the way you did to get some pussy when Lexi was right here!" I snapped as I stood to my feet. I was grilling the fuck out of Phat. I wanted him to give me a reason to reach out and touch him. "You didn't think to wash ya dick off before you brought ya lil dawg ass back here Phat?!" I asked and his mouth dropped. Chris looked between Phat and I like he was trying to figure out what was going.

"Chill out man," Chris said slowly. "Got nothing to do with you," Chris struggled to get out.

"Shut the fuck up Arimaspi! Hobble ya lil cripple ass back to da bed and mind yo damn business!" I snapped at Chris.

They both sat there looking at me like I was one the crazy. "Fuck both of y'all!" I yelled as I walked out the door.

"The fuck is a Arimaspi?" I heard Phat ask.

I turned right back around. "It's exactly what he is right now! A one eyed thief!" I said as I pointed at Chris. "And I don't even know what the fuck to call your triflin' ass right now! But you better take a shower before you go near Alexis nigga!" I said to Phat. I stood there and rubbed my temples because I wanted to attack them both and it was taking everything in me not to.

"Listen V, it ain't what you thinking forreal," Phat said, holding his hands up like he was surrendering.

"I'm not the one you need to be explaining anything to. I didn't ask for a lie nigga!" I said to him.

"Bitch, ain't nobody gotta lie to you!" he yelled back and I ran at him full speed.

He jumped up and swung but he was too slow. I slid between his legs and reached up and grabbed the back of his shirt to pull myself up. As soon as I was standing behind him, I jabbed him directly behind his collarbone, which caused him to fall to the ground. I jumped on top of his chest to karate chop him in the neck.

"Nessa NOOOOO!" Alexis screamed from behind me. I lowered my hand and stood to my feet. I looked at Chris and he was shaking his head at me. Phat sat up slowly and massaged his shoulders. "Are you ok?" Alexis asked as she ran to his side. She wasn't there ten seconds before she slapped the shit out of him. He didn't even have time to answer her question. "How could you?" Alexis asked as she stood to her feet. I could see her eyes watering and if she shed one tear, I was going back into attack mode.

"Lexi!" I called her name firmly. She looked at me with her eyelids brimmed with tears. I shook my head no, letting her know if she cried she wouldn't be able to stop me. Hell, he wouldn't be able to stop me and Chris for damn sure wouldn't be able to stop me. She closed her eyes tightly and took a deep breath.

"Let's go," she said to me and headed towards the door.

"Baby!"

"Don't!" I said as I cut Phat off. If looks could kill, I'd be dead but too bad for Phat, they can't kill you. I turned back around because my purse and keys were on the nightstand. I grabbed them and headed out the front door.

As soon as I stepped out of the door, I saw three females walking up the sidewalk like they were coming here. As I got closer to the road, I saw it was the chick that was here for Chris and two other chicks I had never seen before. The familiar looking chick whispered something to the other girls and they all looked at me like I was on their shit lists!

"Problem?" I asked as I looked dead at them.

"Brittany, what are you doing here? I know Chris didn't call you," Alexis said as she walked up to me and tried to intervene.

"Chris ain't the only one that calls," Brittany replied with a smirk.

I began to mentally put two and two together. First of all, four niggas live here. One dead as fuck and two of them are incapable of calling her. The only one left is the one that just got back smelling like sex. I slid my hand into my pocket, sliding my brass knuckles back on and took a step towards her, only for Alexis to put her hand in front of my chest.

"What you doing?" she whispered towards me.

"This the bitch Phat just fucked!" I said and we both looked at Brittany, who still had that stupid smirk on her face. Alexis attacked her, clawing at her face and pulling her hair. "Slam that bitch on the ground Lexi!" I said as I coached her because this is her first fight. She grabbed Brittany's legs but dropped her. It didn't matter because she was on the ground anyway. "Beat her head in!" I said to Alexis, and she turned and looked at me like I was crazy. I could tell she didn't want to fight.

One of Brittany's friend made a move at Alexis, but I saw her and pulled Alexis out the way, which caused the girl to stumble and fall next to Brittany. That's what happens when you hesitate. If you gone hit a bitch, just do it or someone like me will come along and hit you just for trying her friend. I looked both girls in the eyes and waited on one of them to move. "Go back inside Lexi," I said to her. I couldn't make sure they didn't jump on her while fighting another one.

"I'm not leaving you!" she said and stood behind me.

"Go in the house!" I said through gritted teeth without turning my back on these bitches in front of me. I could hear Alexis suck her teeth as she walked away. I glanced towards the apartment door and as soon as she entered, I dropped down low and spin kicked the one that was about to hit Alexis. The other chick watched her fall when she should have been watching me. I punched her as hard as I could in the face with my brass knuckles on. Brittany started sliding away from me as she shook her head. "No what bitch? Did you tell Phat no?" I asked as I took a step towards her.

"I'm not trying to have no problems with you," she said as she slid back. She grabbed a handful of dirt and threw it my face. It burned the fuck out of my eyes instantly. I couldn't see a thing and I began to hyperventilate. Someone jumped on my back but somehow I managed to flip her off. I heard Brittany groaning, so she must have landed on her. I tried to open my eyes but I still couldn't see. Someone kicked me in the stomach and sent me flying backwards. I didn't have time to react because they were all kicking me over and over all over my body. I grabbed someone's foot and twisted it backwards, breaking it instantly. She groaned out in pain as she fell backwards.

"Man, what the fuck?!" I heard Phat yell before the kicking stopped. I still couldn't see a thing as Alexis helped me to my feet.

Alexis

I've been through so much with men that I just don't want to date anymore. I took a chance with him and he ended up doing me the same way. If that wasn't bad enough, he did it with someone everyone sleeps with! I simply just cannot believe him. The only reason I stopped Vanessa was because I knew she would kill him, and I didn't want him dead. Well, not right then anyway. I wasn't too sure about it after I found out who he slept with.

I was already hurt but looking at that stupid expression on her face sent me into attack mode. I've never been in a fight, not even with my siblings. I've never had to because I'm pretty good at making you think I can fight by the way I talk to you. I'll snap so fast but honestly, my bark is way worse than my bite. I just simply don't have it in me. There I was, attacking someone who helped hurt me and I couldn't even bash her head into the ground like Vanessa said. I was so glad she was telling me what to do because my mind went blank. I kind of changed my mind about the fight the first time my hand connected with her face but I knew it was too late.

When Vanessa broke it up, I could have kissed her because I was so tired. It wasn't until one of Brittany's friends fell that I realized she was stopping her from jumping on me. I didn't want to leave Vanessa when she told me to go inside because I didn't want her to kill anyone. I know you're thinking about Ms. Jackson but that was a birthday present and that lady had been giving her hell all of her life, so it's different.

Reluctantly, I walked in the house to get Phat to stop whatever was about to happen. When I walked in, he was sitting on the couch in the living room with his head in his hands. "Phat, I need you to come outside," I said and he hopped up without question while he pled for forgiveness.

"Baby, I'm sorry. Please under-"

I stopped him by putting my hand in his face. "Come outside now!" I said without looking at him.

"Man y'all might as well go ahead and make up. Y'all getting on my nerves," Chris said as he leaned against the wall for support as he made his way into the living room.

"Man, forget all that! The bitch y'all like to fuck is outside about to fight Vanessa," I said with an attitude.

"Shit, Phat said she killed them niggas over in Newark, so why you in here worried about her fighting a female? And who is she?" Chris asked and pissed me off. They're missing the whole point!

"If she kills Brittany and her friends, someone over here may snitch! I don't want my best friend going to jail over your jump-off!" I yelled, finally looking at Phat.

He walked passed me and headed out the door. "Oh shit." I heard him say, which caused me to turn and run out behind him. Seeing Vanessa laid out on the ground being kicked by those bitches scared me half past dead. I was wondering how they got the jump on her and wished I hadn't left her. Phat walked all the way up to them and pushed Brittany down and pulled the other one away from Vanessa. When I looked closer, I could see the third girl was already on the ground crying and holding her leg. "What the fuck?" Phat said angrily as I began to help Vanessa up. She had dirt all over her face and in her hair. When she stood up completely, she gripped her side tightly while she groaned in pain.

"What the hell you over here for?" I heard Phat asking.

"So, I can't come over here now?" Brittany asked and Vanessa stopped in her tracks. I felt her adjusting her arm and knew she was about to throw a star or a throwing knife.

"Don't," I said and yanked her arm back. She looked at me with pure disgust and if she wasn't in so much pain, I would have let her go. Phat cheating on me broke my heart but the look she just gave me crushed it.

I helped her in the living room where Chris was sitting and walked back out the door. Phat and Brittany were in a heated argument as I walked passed them and headed up the street to hail a cab. They were so into their argument that neither of them noticed I had walked passed.

When I got to the corner, a cab was pulling up. I hopped in, gave him my address, and headed home. Normally, cabbies talk to you or play music but this one did neither one. When I told him my address, he just nodded his head and pulled off.

Forty-five minutes later, we pulled up to the brownstone I share with my sister, April. "It will get better. The heart heals itself, it's the mind that's tricky," the cabbie said to me. I gave him a head nod before I closed the door.

"You finally found your way home huh?" April said from the living room. I glanced at her and noticed the place hadn't been cleaned since the last time I cleaned it. I ignored her and headed up to my room. As soon as I walked in my room, I got pissed off! There was a pizza box on my bed and clothes everywhere! That means that once April contaminated everything else here, she came to the only clean place left, my room!

Without thinking, I stormed down the stairs and walked straight up to April. "What's your problem? Why are you so damn nasty? This is why Jerry moved out!" I screamed. She stood up and pushed me, which caused me to trip over a shoe and land in something unidentifiable. When I looked up at her, she was smiling at me, which made me angrier! I hopped up and dove at her only for her to move out of the way and cause me to hit the chair she was sitting in and flip over it. I was so mad that tears began to fall freely down both cheeks.

"What the hell you always crying for?" April asked she smiled again. I'm so tired of her always laughing at me. Every time I've ever gotten a new boyfriend, she would tell me it wouldn't last. I'd do everything I could think of to keep them but she was always right. When I'd come home brokenhearted, she'd laugh at me and say she told me so.

I stood to my feet slowly with my head down as I walked passed her. I heard her chuckle lightly and that was the straw that broke the camel's back. I turned around and hit her as hard as I could in her face. She hit the floor and was out like a light. I breathed a sigh of relief. It felt so good to knock April on her ass after all of these years. I grabbed her and put her in the chair she was sitting in, so I could clean the house. After I made sure she was out, I decided to start in my room. It took me four hours to clean and sanitize everything, including April's room. I also washed everything and put them up before I showered and crawled in the bed. I decided to check my phone but there were no missed calls or text messages from anyone.

I was in the best sleep I've had in a long time when I was drenched in ice cold water. I mean literally! I jumped up so high, I fell out the bed. It felt like my heart was about to beat out my chest. "You thought you were going to hit me and go to sleep, and I wouldn't retaliate," April said to me. I could tell she was pissed because she didn't smirk afterwards. I stared at her breathing heavily because I was freezing. I was waiting on her to make a move but she didn't. She just turned around and walked out of my room, leaving the bucket she filled with ice water on the floor. I took my wet clothes off and undressed my bed. I headed to the laundry room butt naked with everything in my hands. I decided to wash my covers and sheets first, since I was really tired and just wanted to go back to bed.

After I started the load, I headed back to my room, but made a stop at the bathroom to dry off. Once I finished, I walked with my head held high back to my room. I felt someone staring at me and when I looked up, the guy looked familiar but I couldn't place his face at the moment. I picked up my pace, doing a light jog to my room before I closed and locked the door. I grabbed my other comforter set and redressed my bed completely before I laid down and drifted back off to sleep.

Steve

I woke up with my head killing me because it was hurting so bad. I opened my eyes slowly and looked around the dimly lit cement room. I was on the floor in the corner with my hands cuffed behind my back. There were two guys yelling by the bars. 1 laid across the bench and 1 sat on the toilet. It didn't take me long to realize I was in jail but I was curious to know why I was the only person handcuffed.

I sat up straight and felt, dizzy and lightheaded so I leaned back against the wall. "Guard!" I yelled as loud as I could, bringing unwanted attention to myself.

"Princess has finally woken up." the guy on the bench said as he sat up and looked at me.

"Guard!" I yelled, while I ignored him. I leaned forward and attempted to get up but the room started to spin and I fell back down.

"Someone did a number on you, boy. What you do to him?" the guy asked as he sat on the toilet. I couldn't think of anything other than the fact that this man was talking to me and shitting at the same time. I mean, who does that? I've been through a lot going from foster home to foster home until I finally got to that group home, but never have I ever had to talk to someone while they were actively shitting.

"Guard!" I yelled again and leaned forward. I rocked sideways to get on my knees, so I could stand up. Once I was able to stand, it felt like the room was spinning harder. I could feel my body swaying, so I sat on the bench. Everybody was watching me and probably wondering what the hell happened to me, but I was wondering the same thing. A few minutes later, this big black cop walked over to the cage and unlocked the bars. The two guys that were standing there took a step back to allow him entrance into the holding cell. Without saying a word, he grabbed me roughly and escorted me out of the cell and into an interrogation room. He pushed me down in the chair and walked back out of the room.

They left me in this room alone for what felt like hours before someone finally walked in. "I'm Detective Smith. You've been out for quite a few hours now. Can I get you something?" Detective Smith asked before he took a seat in front of me.

I took a moment to take in her features. She's Hispanic and shaped like a goddess! Wearing black slacks, a white button up and her hair pulled back into a tight ponytail, I could tell she gave these men a run for their money. "What's your name?" she asked, breaking my train of thought. I didn't respond right away because I was admiring her curvy figure. She wore her clothes a size or two bigger, more than likely to hide her figure from male coworkers for more respect. Clearing her throat, she placed a red folder on the table between us.

"What's your name?" Detective Smith asked again.

"Why am I here?" I asked as I finally looked up into her hazel eyes. I have no idea why I looked into her eyes because now I'm sitting here looking at her with my mouth open, falling in love with her. She placed different crime scene photos in front of me, one at a time and each of a different body. I stared at the pictures as I began to remember everything that happened earlier tonight.

My blood began to boil as I thought about how Chris, Frankie, and that bitch jumped on me and left me for dead! It's because of them that I'm sitting in an interrogation room with seven pictures of dead bodies in front of me. "Why'd you do it?" Detective Smith asked.

"I didn't do anything. Am I under arrest?" I asked her.

"No, you're not, but I have a few more questions," she answered me.

"Why am I handcuffed then?" I asked. Instead of responding, she got up to free my wrists before she sat back down. "I don't have any answers. I don't even remember nothing!" I said to her. I didn't kill nobody and I was not going down for killing nobody either.

"So, you don't remember killing all of these people?" she asked me with her head tilted to the side.

"Man, I didn't kill nobody!" I screamed at her because she was really starting to piss me off.

"How do you know if you don't remember?" she asked as she squinted her eyes at me.

"I want a lawyer," I said as I sat back in the chair and crossed my arms across my chest.

"If you didn't do anything, you don't need a lawyer. Besides, you aren't under arrest," she said with a simple shrug of the shoulder.

"So, I can get up and walk out of here?" I asked her, as I rubbed my hands up and down my thighs and dried them off. I didn't realize I was sweating profusely until this very second. I know she's thinking I'm guilty but at the same time, she knows she found me unconscious.

"Yes. We will be keeping an eye on you," she said and gathered the pictures off of the table. I stood to my feet and walked out of the door.

Once I was outside, I felt the vomit rising as I bent over where I stood and puked everywhere. "Regret got you feeling woozy?" I heard someone ask from behind me. I turned around and stood face to face with another detective. I only knew he was a detective because he had a chain around his neck with his badge as the charm. I just shook my head before I used my sleeve to wipe my mouth. As I descended the steps, I still felt his presence behind me. "Can I give you a lift?" he asked.

It was then that I realized I had nowhere to go. Even though the apartment is rightfully mines, I can't just walk in after what I did. "Man, who are you?" I asked the detective.

"I'm Detective Broughton," he said with his hand extended to shake mine. For some reason, I began to trust him immediately. "Do you have somewhere to go?" Detective Broughton asked me.

I looked down at the ground and shook my head. "Well, my daughter is about to move out and my son moved out yesterday. She's hardly ever home, so you can crash at my place until you find something," he said to me.

The fact that he's offering his place to a possible murderer is a little fishy but since I have nowhere else to go, I agreed. We hopped in his unmarked car and headed to his home. When we pulled up, it was a nice little brownstone. There were no family pictures anywhere and I began to get nervous. After noticing my hesitation, he stopped and looked at me. "What's wrong?" he asked as he gestured for me to have a seat.

"No pictures?" I asked while I looked around the living room.

"We use to take tons of pictures before my wife passed away. After that, we just didn't need the reminders of what was," Detective Broughton explained. "Let me show you where you will be staying," he said as he stood and walked out of the living room. I followed behind him passed his daughter's room, on down the hall to the room right across from his. This is the first time I'd have my own room!

"What's your name?" Detective Broughton asked.

"Steve," I answered as I shook his hand.

"I'm Michael," he said before he walked away.

Vanessa

I can't believe I let them bitches get the best of me. Never in my life would I have imagined that after all I've done, I'd get my ass handed to me by three simple females. Do you know how many animals I've killed? Do you know how many strangers I've killed that no one knows about? I tell Alexis a lot but you should never let your left hand know what your right hand is doing. I've been killing animals and people since my mom died. It started off with squirrels and random animals that wouldn't be missed. When that wasn't enough for me, I decided to get joy off killing animals that meant something to someone, so I started killing pets in our neighborhood. I chose our neighborhood because I wanted to see their reaction. I could have gone across town to kill pets but I would never know how they felt. Pretty soon, I was able to trick my brother Wayne into setting traps for homeless people, so I could kill them. He knows what I do when I'm alone, which is why he's always asking me where I'm going or where I've been. I'm pretty sure when I showed up with my face bruised up after Chris and I fight, he thought I was trying to kill someone and almost lost. See, I know he's worried I'm going to get myself killed, which is why I have to move out. If we aren't living together then he won't know when I'm home or not, and he won't be worried about me anymore.

Anyway, I could hear Brittany asking Phat whether or not it was okay if she came over or not, so I knew Alexis could hear as well. I was about to end her by throwing one of my stars and hitting her dead between the eyes but Alexis stopped me. Her weakness really disgusted me! I don't understand how or why she allowed people to blatantly disrespect her the way they do. I wish my so called man would come around me smelling like sex and just walk away! He'd be lucky if he survives the beating I'm going to give him. I know Alexis wasn't going to do anything to Phat, yet she stopped me from teaching him a lesson. She knows me well so she had to know I was about to lay her competition out, but she stopped me! I don't understand at all but that's my best friend and I'll do anything to protect her, so Brittany better watch her back!

Alexis helped me inside and the first thing I saw was Chris' hard headed ass sitting on the couch watching TV. Once I was seated, Alexis walked right back out of the door. Chris and I shared a confused glance before he started laughing. "What's funny?" I asked as I rotated my body, so I'd be facing him.

"How the hell you kill three niggas and get your ass beat by three bitches?" he asked still laughing, which caused me to laugh as well.

"You win some and you lose some. But you live, you live to breathe and fight another day!" I said as I gave my best impression of Pops off the movie *Friday*. Chris started laughing so hard that he started coughing and before long, he was choking. I stood up to fix him some water but could barely stand on my own because my side was hurting so bad. I lost my balance before I made it to the kitchen and fell on the floor laughing so hard that I started crying.

"Man, you can't do shit right!" Chris said and stood up to help me. He grabbed my arm and helped me stand to my feet with both of us groaning in pain.

"Let's go watch Pretty Little Liars," I suggested as we held each other up. He smiled at me as we stumbled our way into his room, using the walls for support.

Once we made it into his room, we no longer had the walls to hold onto so we used each other. The problem with that was neither of us could stand on our own and we both ended up falling. Chris hit the floor first and knocked the wind out of himself. I was able to rotate my body, so I wouldn't fall on the side that was sore. I looked over at Chris as he tried to catch his breath and the sight was just so funny! I started laughing so hard that it was making my side hurt worse.

"What the hell y'all in here doing?" Phat asked, as he stood in the door shaking his head.

"Trying to watch Pretty Little Liars," I answered, still laughing and grabbing my side.

"I outta kick you in yo shit for fighting me earlier," Phat said as he smiled at me.

"Well, technically, you swung first. Plus, if you hit me now, you better kill me," I said with a serious expression on my face.

He didn't respond, he just walked over to me and scooped scooping me up in his arms and tossed me on Chris' bed. The shit hurt so bad but I didn't even say anything because I was just glad I was in the bed. I watched as he helped Chris stand to his feet and helped him in the bed as well.

"Aye, don't forget to put another chair behind the door in case Steve comes while we're asleep," I said.

"Fuck! I was fina go get Lexi. I can't let her be alone to think about the shit. I ain't even really fuck the girl like talking bout it," Phat said while he shook his head and confused me. How do you not really have sex with someone? I don't even know what he's talking about right now.

"Gone get her. I got my stars and knives. Just close and lock Chris' door, so if he comes in here, we have a chance to wake up," I said as I tried not to think about the amount of stupidity that just came out his mouth.

"Want a massage?" Chris asked as soon as we heard the front door close. I looked at him sideways because I was thinking about the last massage he gave me. He smiled slightly, so I already knew he was going to try something I'm not ready for.

"Do you have sex a lot?" I asked him curiously.

He looked at me strangely before turning his attention to the tv. Instead of prying, I started watching tv as well. "Yes," he said without looking away from the TV.

"Oh," I said simply, which caused him to look at me.

"Oh?" he asked and sat up.

"Yeah, oh. I was just curious," I said without looking at him.

"Why were you curious?" he asked and I could feel his eyes burning holes through the side of my face. I began to think of ways to tell him why I was curious. I figured I couldn't go wrong with the truth.

"I'm a virgin," I said after I turned to look at him.

"Bullshit!" he said as he looked at me like he just knows I'm lying. Instead of arguing about something I couldn't prove, I just turned back towards the tv to watch.

Knock, Knock

"Fuck!" Chris said as he looked at me.

"What?" I asked confused.

"Damn door locked! Go open it," he said as he shoved me softly.

"Shitting me! This your room," I said as I frowned up at him.

"Who is it?" Chris yelled.

"Frankie," she answered with a shaky voice.

I watched as Chris slowly stumbled to the door. As soon as he unlocked it, it burst open and slammed into the wall, which caused the door knob to create a big hole in the wall. Thinking fast, I rolled off the other side of the bed and landed on my hands. I slithered my body underneath the bed and pulled myself up, just in case they looked under the bed I wouldn't be seen.

I couldn't see any faces but I counted out ten feet, four of which belonged to Chris and Frankie. "Who in here with you?" I heard someone ask. The voice sounded familiar but I couldn't place it.

"I'm sorry Chris. They grabbed me coming through the front door," Frankie said, which pissed me off. She need to learn how to stand her ground and protect herself. How stupid can you be not to watch your back after people you considered family turned on you? Yes, one of them is dead but we have no idea where the other one is.

"It's cool sis," Chris responded to her.

Ring, Ring

"Fuck!" I said under my breath. My work phone was ringing and even if these dumb mufuckers weren't in the way of stopping my money, I'm still hurting and probably wouldn't be able to do the job right now anyway.

"Where's the phone?" I heard the familiar voice ask. "Find it!" he yelled after no one answered him. I have no idea where my purse is but I know if they find it, they'd find my i.d., which is in my wallet. I can't have them finding my work phone either. I could hear things being tossed around, then a gun was cocked.

"Where you think you going pretty boy?" someone asked Chris.

"Don't pull out no gun if you ain't gone use it. Bitches coming in here messing my damn room up and shit!" Chris snapped. I really can't believe this man getting this mad about his damn room, like they don't have guns.

POW

I heard a gun go off and it scared the fuck out of me. I peeked out and nobody was on the ground. "Next time, I won't miss," the shooter said. These got to be amateurs coming in here and not knowing who they're messing with. I could see feet headed towards the bed.

"Man, don't sit on my damn bed!" Chris snapped, then I heard a light chuckle. If I've learned anything about Chris, it's that his ass don't play about his bed. I know he's not going to let anyone sit on it. As crazy as it sounds, I know he doesn't care about anybody having guns on him either. I have to plan this and time it just right for it to work.

Phat

Standing in Chris' doorway watching him and Vanessa's crippled ass trying to help the other make it to the bed was indeed a sight to see. I wanted to laugh but thoughts of Alexis began to fill my mind. I can't let her go home thinking something happened that didn't happen. I did fuck her but not how Alexis thinking I did. See, I know Alexis and I know she's thinking that I shared the kind of moments with Brittany that I share with her but it ain't that kind of party. That's why I told Vanessa I didn't fuck Brittany like talking about it. I didn't miss the look she gave me and I know she was dismissing me the way she told me to go ahead and get her. The only thing is, I know this is not the time to leave them alone. Under different circumstances, it would be fine. By different circumstances, I mean by them both being injured and the fact that we don't know if Steve is alive or not. I walked out the door and remembered Frankie will be back soon because she just went to the store.

Walking down the street to catch a cab, my mind began to drift back to talking to Brittany after breaking up the fight.

"What are you doing here?!" I asked with an attitude.

"I can't come over here now?" Brittany asked as she snaked her neck at me. I looked at Alisha on the ground nursing her ankle and thought that's what the fuck she gets for jumping on Vanessa like that.

"Cut the bullshit man, what you want?" I asked clearly irritated.

"I want to know if I'm pregnant, will we be a family?" Brittany asked, like I nutted in her two or more months ago when it has barely been two or more hours. I turned around and made sure Alexis hadn't heard any of that and luckily, she was in the house by then.

"What, you scared your weak ass girlfriend heard her?" Stephanie asked me.

"Bitch, shut the fuck up, ain't nobody talking to yo maggot ass!" I snapped, ready to slap fire from her.

"Baby, the way you talking making me horny. Want to come back to my place? I mean the harm is already done, you

might as well get it out your system," Brittany said seductively, which made my dick jump. She reached her small hand out and massaged my dick, and I let her until I heard the door close, which snapped me back into reality.

"Keep your fucking hands and mouth to your damn self! Don't bring y'all ass back around here either!" I snapped as I yelled in her face.

"Nigga, fuck you! I know if you don't call, Chris gone call so you better believe you will be seeing me! And nigga, if this baby is yours, you gone be seeing a lot of me!" she screamed and caused me to check my surroundings again. I looked down the street and saw Alexis speed walking to the corner. I hope like hell she heard none of that shit Brittany was just spitting because I don't want to lose her.

"Man, fuck you! You ain't even pregnant man. As a matter of fact, here!" I snapped and peeled off eight 20's then handed it to her. "Go get a fucking plan B and take care of that shit!" I snapped.

"And if I don't?" she asked as she sucked her teeth.

"If you don't, I'm going to get Vanessa and trust me, she ain't gone let y'all get the best of her twice," I said to her.

I watched a cab pull up, so I headed over to it but when she saw me coming, she pulled off. I guess she thought I was about to rob her. I continued around the corner when this all black Tahoe truck almost hit me because it was turning so fast. I had to dive out the way to avoid being hit. When I sat up, I noticed the lady in the cab watching me. I stood up and headed straight to her but she pulled off. I rounded the corner and hailed a cab to Alexis' house.

When I got outside the door, I almost punked out. I sat on the porch for so long that my butt cheeks were asleep. When I stood up to stretch, my legs were stiff. I turned the doorknob and it was unlocked. I walked in and looked around at how clean everything was, so I know Alexis was pissed. See, Alexis only cleaned up like this when she's mad or hurt. I walked slowly through the house and I could hear light moans coming from up the stairs. I took off towards Alexis' room and burst in, only to find her fast asleep with her foot hanging off the bed. I adjusted her body and cuddled under the covers with her falling asleep instantly.

Alexis

I woke up wishing the pain I felt from the betrayal of my love was all a dream. When I tried to stretch out, I smelled his cologne and hopped out the bed. Stealing a page out of April's book, I walked downstairs and filled the bucket up with ice and water. When I was walking back out of the kitchen, April was leaning against the wall in the hallway. "Thought you were gonna get me back huh?" she asked and smiled at me. I winked at her before walking past her and back up the stairs. I could hear her trailing behind me being nosey. When I got back to my room, I realized the door was off the hinges, meaning this nigga broke his way into my damn room!

"Hold it high so you can get all of him," April said as she grinned from ear to ear. I held the bucket as high as I could and dumped it on him. He woke up swinging and one of his licks caught me in the stomach, which caused me to double over in pain before I fell on the floor. "What the fuck going on?" he asked, looking crazy and trying to catch his breath. I looked up at him with tears streaming down my face. "Oh shit, baby! I'm sorry," he said as he got on his knees next to me.

"Here y'all go with the mushy shit. Save me!" April said and walked away from my room.

"You're right, you are sorry! Why are you here?" I asked, mad that my plan to get him backfired and I ended up hurt again.

Phat stood to his feet before he reached his hand out for mine. I reluctantly gave it to him. After pulling me up, he walked to the bed and undressed it completely before he grabbed my hands and the dirty linen and headed towards the laundry room. When he opened the washing machine, he looked at me quizzically.

"Long story," I said as I pulled everything out to put in the dryer. When I finished, he was loading the washing machine with my other bedding. He grabbed my hand again and led me to living room. "Ask me anything and I'm going to be honest and explain in a way I hope you understand and forgive me," he said as he knelt in front of me.

I took a seat on the couch and thought of what I wanted to ask, but at the same time I wondered if I really wanted to know. I love this man and I know he loves me, so I'm willing to give him one more chance. "If you cheat on me again, I'm going to let Nessa kill you," I said with a serious expression on my face. Instead of responding, he pulled me up into his arms. He was soaked and wet, and I didn't even care. "Let's go back to your house," I suggested and his eyes began to smile. You ever look at someone and can tell just by looking in their eyes that they're happy? Well, his eyes told me all his secrets. I can always tell how he's feeling by looking in his eyes.

I led the way back into my room where I found April standing there and shaking her head. "I can't believe we're related. This nigga hurt ya lil stupid ass and all he had to do was break in your house and let you pour water on him," she said as she grilled me and shook her head. "If he will cheat once, then he will cheat twice. Keep accepting it and watch you be back here cleaning up after me more and more," she continued then walked passed me and bumped into Phat on her way out.

"She's wrong," he said.

"I know because if you cheat on me again, Vanessa will kill you," I said before I found me something to wear.

After getting dressed and handling my personal hygiene, we were headed out the door. I flagged down a cab as I waited for Phat to come outside. The female cabbie was just sitting there and staring at me, probably wondering what was taking me so long. I couldn't really see her face but she looked so familiar, but I couldn't place her. When Phat walked out of the door she pulled off. I turned and looked at him strangely.

"What?" Phat asked.

"Nothing. I'm tripping," I said as we walked down the street to try and catch a cab.

It took forever for us to hail a cab but when we did, we couldn't keep our hands off each other. After pulling up to where Phat lived, we kissed all the way to the door. When he opened the door, it smelled so bad inside! Frankie was asleep on the couch and I was wondering where Vanessa and Phat were. "Frankie. Frankie. Wake up," Phat said and shook her out her sleep. I watched in slow motion as she pulled out a gun and started firing.

Chris

Spending time with Vanessa is always good, even with both of us hurting the way we are. Now when Frankie knocked on the door, I didn't want to get up but I'm glad it was me and not Vanessa. I know she's faster with the shit she throws from a distance. She may be a killing machine but she just got her ass handed to her because she was trying not to kill them. There's no doubt in my mind that she can kill all three of these mufuckers but considering I had no idea where her little ass ran off to that fast, I don't know what to think. These niggas made one mistake though, they should have come in blasting but since they didn't, they will die.

"I'm sorry Chris. They grabbed me coming through the front door," Frankie said to me. I was really pissed off that she could be so careless at a time like this. Anytime someone close to you betrayed you the way we've been betrayed, you should automatically put your guard up. What sense do it make walking around like everything is all watermelon and rainbows?

"It's cool sis," I responded to her. I really wanted to snap on her but I know now is not the time. Plus, I know she's kicking her own ass mentally for this.

Ring, Ring

"Where's the phone?" one of the guys asked. I just looked at him, trying to figure out why it even fucking matter. They still haven't told me what they're here for and now I'm even more curious. "Find it!" he yelled after I didn't answer him. I looked at Frankie, who was standing there teary eyed, like some damn tears would get us out of this. She was pissing me off and I was wondering how the fuck she been robbing niggas with us all this time.

I have no idea where the phone was but watching them mess my room up had my blood boiling! One of the guys opened my dresser drawer and dumped all of my things out on the floor. That was it for me as I took a step closer to him to knock his ass out but hearing a gun cock stopped me dead in my tracks. "Where you think you going, pretty boy?" one of the guys asked me.

"Don't pull out no gun if you ain't gone use it. Bitches coming in here messing my damn room up and shit!" I snapped because I wanted to kill all of them with my bare hands. I don't give a fuck about no damn guns they not using! If they came here to kill us, we would be dead already! I'll be damned if I'm about to sit around like a bitch and let these niggas punk me like this.

POW

The shooter shot the gun in my direction trying to scare me. I grilled the fuck out of him because if he wanted to get a point across, he should have shot me or Frankie. Hell, what's shooting that damn wall going to do? "Next time I won't miss," the shooter said. It took everything in me not to laugh at this wanna be gangsta ass nigga. If he was really bout it, I wouldn't have tried him in the first place. Well, I would have but there wouldn't have been a shadow of doubt that I'd be dead shortly after.

While one guy was dumping my clothes on the floor, I saw the other one headed towards my bed. By then, the phone had stopped ringing and they were just tossing everything around like the feds. Out the corner of my eye, I could see one of the guys walking to my bed. "Man, don't sit on my damn bed!" I snapped and he laughed a little bit. If this nigga thought I was going to let him get on my bed, he had another thing coming. I glanced over at Frankie and the tears were falling freely, and she was shaking her head telling me no. Fuck that! The guy looked at me and winked before taking another step towards my bed. I'm about to fuck dude up and the only thing that was going to stop me was a bullet to the head.

As soon as he got within arm's reach of my bed, I hit him and grabbed his shirt so he wouldn't fall on my bed. I heard the gun go off again but I didn't care. I hit dude about four times before I pulled his mask off. I had no idea who he was. "Is he dead?" Vanessa asked, which caused me to look up. It was then I noticed that nobody joined in to help him fight. As I looked up at her breathing slightly heavy, I could feel myself falling deeper in love with her. Looking down at the floor, I saw the other two guys laid out dead. One with a knife between his eyes and the other with them damn stars in both ankles and one in his mouth. I looked back up at Vanessa as she shrugged her shoulders.

"Move out the way," Vanessa said and pushed me, so she could check his pulse. "Frankie, get me something to tie him up with," Vanessa said but Frankie was just standing there staring off into space. I watched Vanessa clench her fist and knowing her, she's going to hit her.

"What's wrong Frankie?" I asked her as I stood up next to her.

"I'm so sorry. I wasn't paying attention and I should have been," she cried.

"Oh, should've, could've, would've, but guess what Frankie? You didn't! We could have been killed but guess what Frankie? We're still here! Get the fuck over yourself and go get something for me to tie him up with!" Vanessa yelled with no sympathy at all. She got me wondering if she's capable of feeling anything other than anger. I mean I've seen her laugh but I've seen her mad more than I've seen her happy. Granted, I haven't known her that long but damn.

"You didn't have to talk to her like that," I said to Vanessa as I tried to reason with her. She shot me a look that would shut anybody up but me. "Man, don't look at me like that. You the only one brought up with no struggle. You walk around this bitch mad at the world because your mom died like you weren't still blessed!" I snapped at her because she was pissing me off.

"Oh, shut the fuck up! Your parents ain't give a fuck about you and neither did hers, and that's the only reason you're jumping down my throat now. I guess if my parents didn't care about me, what I said would have been ok, huh? So had Phat said it, it would be fine, right?" She snapped right back and fucked my mind up. I honestly didn't know what to say to her. I stood up and left out of the room just when Frankie was coming back with duct tape.

Vanessa

I've realized that people are just too sensitive to deal with my mouth. A lot of people simply can't handle someone who's right in your face with how they feel but that's me. If I fuck with you, I promise you will know it and if I don't, then you will feel it. I don't have time to sugar coat anything. What's the point in me walking on eggshells to protect your feelings when you're going to take it exactly how you want to anyway?

I take things exactly for what they are without trying to change it to make it better for me. I've always been an 'it is what it is' type of person. Just like when I was holding myself up under the bed, so those men wouldn't see me and kill me. My ribs are still killing me but I'm alive! When I knew Chris wouldn't let someone get on his bed, as dumb as it sounds, I knew he would risk his life to stop it from happening. I'm a fast thinker so it's because of me that we are alive.

I timed Chris perfectly, lowering myself and throwing stars before I rolled from under the opposite side of the bed. The first guy didn't know what hit him as he bent over about to pull the stars out his ankles. The other guy was looking dead at me but just as I expected, they were amateurs. He was staring at me in shock when he should have been shooting me. He deserved to die for watching me throw a knife at his face. The only logical thing for him to do was to kill me first but he was stuck on stupid, the same way Frankie was! So, excuse the fuck out of me if I have no sympathy for stupidity. In life, you have to always pay attention to your surroundings because it's always a matter of life and death. Don't ever think it's not that simple because it is. Every move you make in these streets could be the reason you're dead or the reason you're still breathing.

At first, I thought Chris could handle my mouth but after I snapped back after he tried to get me together, he just walked out the room. It's like damn, can I get everybody to leave their feelings in their pocket while we figure out who the fuck this nigga is and who sent them?

"Here," Frankie said and tossed a roll of duct tape next to me on the floor. I looked at her but decided not to say anything. Hey, maybe she thought my hands were hurting, so she threw the tape on the floor. I don't care though. I understand she's in her feelings because she's always in her damn feelings.

"Can you bring a chair in your room for me?" I asked Frankie, who looked at me crazy. "Well, since it's your fault they came in and almost killed us, I figured it was only right that we use your room," I said with a smile. Instead of responding, she walked out of the room. I grabbed his legs and dragged him across the carpet. My chest was on fire; it was hurting so bad! Man, after we get through with this, I'm going to get myself checked out. I moaned and groaned loudly until I got him in the hallway. I slid down the wall into a seated position as I tried to catch my breath.

"You got it?" Chris asked me as he leaned against the wall.

"Yea, piece of cake," I said sarcastically.

"Alright. Let me know if you need me," he said and turned around, which caused me to exhale deeply.

"Don't get slapped Chris, come on!" I said with an attitude. He walked over to me smiling as he grabbed his feet turning him around. "What the hell you doing? We taking him to Frankie's room." I said, which caused him to frown at me.

"It's ok Chris," Frankie said and walked out of her room. "The chair is in my room," Frankie said without looking at me. She walked passed us and headed into the living room.

"Give her a gun and tell her to keep watch or something," I said and shooed Chris away as I stood up.

After he came back around the corner, he grabbed the guy's legs and pulled him all the way in Frankie's room, like he wasn't hurting anymore. "Did you take something?" I asked as I followed him into Frankie's room.

"Naw. Why?" he asked as he looked directly at me. I can't look him in the eyes long because I can feel myself falling for him. The problem is I know nothing about this man to feel the way I feel about him. Well, the things I know will send most females, well smart females, running for the hills but there's something drawing me near him.

"Because you don't seem to be in any pain and not long ago, we could both barely stand up," I said and shied away from his gaze. He picked the guy up from the floor and sat him in the chair before he turned around to look at me. We stared at each other for several seconds before I looked away again.

"Where's the tape?" he asked, which caused me to look around the room. Without a word, I got up and walked swiftly to Chris' room and it was still on the floor where Frankie tossed it. I grabbed it before I headed back into Frankie's room.

I tossed Chris the roll of tape and the guy was getting ready to fall out the chair. By the time Chris noticed what was happening, he was already lying under him. I laughed as I pulled his arm and tried to get him off Chris. I pulled until I heard it pop and he woke up screaming and scared the mess out of me! I jumped back and hit my back on Frankie's dresser before hearing a gun go off. Chris and I shared a glance before he hit the guy again and knocked him back out. I scrambled to my feet and ran towards the living room. When I walked in, there was a guy slumped over and sitting in the doorway. I looked over at a shook up Frankie, still holding the smoking gun and aimed at where he once stood.

Shaking my head, I walked over to the door slowly and peeked out. There was an all-black truck parked a few buildings down that wasn't there when we were outside fighting. Well, at least I don't remember seeing it. I pulled his body all the way inside as Chris was coming down the hall. "What the hell happened?" Chris asked, once he realized I was pulling a body inside the apartment.

"Come help me," I said as I groaned and tried not to grab my side.

Chris walked over to me, picked the guy up, and tossed him over his shoulder like he weighed nothing. "Bring another chair Nessa, he's still breathing!" he yelled on his way to Frankie's room. I grabbed a chair and followed behind him. This fool had done wrapped the tape around the other guy maybe twice, like the man can't simply rock out of the chair and free himself.

"He needs more tape so he can't get loose," I said as I laughed and walked out the room.

"Where you going?" he asked me.

"To check on Frankie," I replied and he smiled at me. I don't know what that was all about.

When I walked back into the living room, Frankie was sitting in the same spot with the door wide open. I walked over to the door and closed and locked it before sitting next to Frankie. I gently placed my hand on top of hers and lowered the gun into her lap before I took it out of her hands. As soon as I took the gun, her hands started trembling. She began to rock back and forth as she held herself. Seconds later, the tears started rolling! She was crying and rocking without making a single sound as I watched her with wide eyes. I had no idea what to do. I've never been in this kind of situation before. I almost hugged her but I don't like people hugging me, so I scooted over in the opposite direction. She still didn't stop crying, so I got up and walked to the bathroom to get some tissue. When I handed her the tissue, she started sobbing so I snatched it back, thinking something was wrong with it. I looked between her and the tissue, wondering what the hell was wrong with her.

I got up and sat on the other couch because my palm was starting to itch, and I knew I would slap her, which may or may not be what she needed at this moment. I can't be sure because I don't know why she's crying. It took her several minutes before the sobs stopped and she started silently crying again. I walked back into the bathroom, looked in the medicine cabinet, and found some Advil PMs. I grabbed three and went into the kitchen to fix her some juice. I crushed the pills up and poured the residue in the glass, stirring it slightly before I walked it over to her.

"Drink this," I said and handed her the glass. She gulped it down without any question. I sat in the living room with her until her eyes started rolling. I pushed her over slightly and she fell right on to sleep. I grabbed her gun and slid it under her hands. I know she didn't need to be sleep but I had something I needed to help Chris with in the back. Plus, I know that if she's scared out of her sleep, she's going to start shooting.

Chris

I could've thumped Vanessa on the forehead for watching that man fall on me. I was trying to put the duct tape around his ankles when his big ass fell out the chair. Then she thought it was funny until she damn near snatched his arm off his body! As soon I heard it pop, I knew he would wake up. He was just screaming though. He didn't try to fight or see what was going on or nothing, just screamed! When we heard the gunshot, I wanted to check it out but I needed to shut his big ass up and get him in the chair first. I felt like Vanessa could read my mind because she did exactly what I wanted her to do, which was make sure Frankie was alright. Frankie is my little sister and I'm falling in love with Vanessa, so I need them to be the same way she and Alexis are. I hit buddy as hard as I could from the position I was in and knocked his ass right back out!

I got him up in the chair and wrapped the duct tape around him enough to hold him up while I made sure everything was ok up front. On my way down the hall, I could see the door was open but I didn't see the body until I walked all the way in the living room. I glanced at Frankie and she was still holding the gun up, like she was making sure no one else was going to come through the door. She was sweating because she was scared as fuck though. It had me wondering what happened to her growing up that got her scared of guns the way she was and how was she so good at something she's afraid of.

I could clearly see Vanessa having a hard time pulling the guy inside but she don't want to need anyone, and I kind of get a kick out of making her ask me for help. I grabbed buddy up and could feel him breathing, so I told Vanessa to bring another chair in the room. She brought the chair to me and left back out to check on Frankie. That alone made me look at her differently. Especially, since I know she's not a sympathetic type of person.

Maybe Frankie needs someone to give her tough love like I know Vanessa will. Hell, we all need somebody like that.

After I taped both guys securely in their chairs, I sat on Frankie's dresser and waited on Vanessa to come back to the room. It took her ass so long that I was starting to doze off when she walked in the room and snapped her fingers in my face. I grabbed her small frame and pulled her close to me, which shocked her and myself when I kissed her. Hell, the fact that she kissed me back shocked me! I could feel my man rising so I pulled away because I had business to handle, plus she think I believe she's a virgin. Ain't nobody our damn age no virgin, so I don't know why she think she can pull the wool over my eyes. When I pulled back, she still had her eyes closed, so I kissed her nose. She looked up at me as we stared in each other's eyes before she looked away.

"I need to run out to my car to get my supplies," she said and ran off before I could respond. She must have parked close because she was back in no time with a book bag. She walked back out of the room and returned with salt. When I looked at her, I'm sure confusion was written all over my face. I watched her check their legs to make sure they were taped securely to the legs of the chair. After that, she tugged them slightly and rocked them by their shoulders before she taped them more. She turned towards me and winked, which caused my dick to jump.

Adjusting my pants, I walked over to where she was. "What you about to do?" I asked as I stood next to her.

"Get some answers," she stated plainly. By the way she responded, I knew shit was about to get real, real fast in here. "Go get two glasses of cold water for me please," she demanded. Normally, I wouldn't go but she had me curious as fuck.

I walked out of the room and headed down the hall when I heard light snores. Peeking into the living room, I noticed Frankie was knocked the fuck out with a gun in her hand. I know she's supposed to be keeping watch but I also know better than to wake someone up that has a gun in their hands. I love Frankie to death but if she shoots me and I live, she won't.

Ignoring Frankie, I walked in the kitchen and poured two glasses of cold water before returning to the room of pain. I handed the glasses over to Vanessa and watched her take a big gulp from one before sitting it on the dresser. She grabbed the other one and threw it in the first guy's face. He woke up breathing hard before he grimaced in pain from his shoulder hanging and looking all types of disfigured. I looked down at Vanessa and she was smiling at him like she knew something we didn't. "Note to self, never get on her bad side," I said out loud to myself. Vanessa looked back at me with a slight smirk before she turned back around.

"What you doing?" he asked as he watched Vanessa move the nightstand next to his chair. Ignoring him, she pulled a wallet out and opened it across the nightstand. It had all kinds of knives of different sizes. I knew she was a knife person but damn.

"What's your name?" Vanessa asked him and squatted in front of him to place her hands on his lap.

"Fuck you bitch!" he snapped, which caused her to laugh at him. She squeezed his leg close to his knee and when I heard a pop, I leaned over so I could get a better view. I was in awe as I looked at this man's kneecap sitting on the side of his leg. I looked at him and he was sweating and crying like a bitch. The sight was pissing me off but I'm glad he didn't start screaming.

"What's your name?" Vanessa asked, as she placed her hand on his other leg. His eyes got as big and as round as saucers.

"Fuck you bitch!" he said with spittle flying from his mouth.

Vanessa turned and looked at me and flashed the brightest smile I'd ever seen. "Toss me a sock babe," she said to me before she turned around. I pulled a sock out of Frankie's drawer and handed it to her. He turned his head to keep her from sticking the sock in his mouth. "Let me explain something to you. What I'm about to do next is going to hurt so bad, you will need this sock in your mouth to help you. See, you're either gonna scream or grit your teeth. If you grit your teeth on top of teeth, you could break them but if you do it on the sock, it will be ok," Vanessa said, explaining it to him as if she was a friend and not the person that was about to torture him. He coughed up as much spit as he could and spat it directly in Vanessa's face.

"That wasn't nice," she said as she stood to her feet and left out the room.

"Who are you?" I asked him, trying my luck.

"Fuck you! I see who calling the shots and it ain't your bitch ass!" he snapped at me, which caused me to chuckle.

"Funny how you're playing hard but soon, you're gonna be begging her to kill you when I know she don't want to kill you my man. All you have to do is answer her questions," I said as I tried to play the nice guy. Before he could respond, Vanessa was walking back into the room with a clean face and a bottle of alcohol and peroxide. "Where you get that from?" I asked her because I know we ain't have that shit here.

"My bag. I stay prepared for this," she answered and turned her attention back to the guy. I watched her pull something out of her pocket and broke it under his nose. Whatever it was made him throw his head back with his mouth wide open and inhale deeply. She stood up fast and stuck the sock deep in his mouth. I hopped down and grabbed his head to hold it still, as she put duct tape over the sock.

"Thanks," she said and smiled up at me. I looked away before I hopped back on the dresser. I watched her stand to her feet and grab a small knife off the nightstand before she sat in front of him. I could feel him looking at me, so I looked in his direction and he was shaking his head no. I gave him a slight shoulder shrug and indicated it's out of my hands. I watched as she took her time and cut layer after layer of skin off his knee. By the time she was able to cut his kneecap out completely, he had done passed out three times. I hopped down to stretch my legs and look at the wound and surprisingly, it wasn't as bloody as you would imagine it would be. I imagined blood all over her, him, and the floor but that isn't at all what it looked like.

"Why you ain't go to school to be a surgeon or some shit?" I asked confused. This girl is smart as hell and gets joy out of killing. I'm not judging her but damn, with her skills, she could go far legally. Hell, she could go further illegally.

"I don't like school. I plan on enrolling in college though, I just don't know what I want to do," she said and grabbed the bottle of peroxide. She poured it over the wound and I watched it sizzle and clean the infection out the wound. He woke up instantaneously and shook his head fast from the pain. It took a few minutes for the peroxide to finish its job but afterwards, she pulled the tape and sock off his mouth. He was breathing extremely fast and heavy.

"Slow your breathing or you will pass out. I don't want to hurt you anymore. All I want is for you to answer a few questions," she said to him in a soft nurturing tone. He looked at me and I nodded my head at him. "What's your name?" she asked him.

"Bo," he said.

"Man, shut the fuck up!" the other guy said, which caused Vanessa and I to look in his direction. I didn't even know he was awake until now.

Vanessa ignored him by returning her attention back to Bo. "Hey Bo. It's nice to meet you. Well, not under these circumstances but hey, God makes no mistakes, right?" Vanessa said to Bo. "I just want to know who sent you to kill me and my friends. That wasn't very nice of them. I mean, we were watching Pretty Little Liars and I think we were about to find out who A was before you guys came barging in the room," she said to him, like they were old friends.

"I don't know man. Just following orders," he said as he shook his head.

"Shut the fuck up Bo! You've already said too much!" the other guy yelled. I hopped off the dresser and knocked him out with an upper cut. The whole chair fell backwards and I had to pick it back up. It was then I realized he was bleeding. It had completely slipped my mind that Frankie shot him coming through the door.

"Aye Babe. Buddy over here losing a lot of blood," I said to Vanessa.

"I'm on it," she said and dug through her bag. She located his gunshot wound right above his waistline then put gloves on. My stomach began to turn as she dug her small fingers in the wound. The guy woke up and was screaming like a bitch until he passed back out. It took her about twenty minutes to get the bullet out. "Lucky you, the bullet didn't break into pieces. See, I don't want to kill y'all. I want to kill the person or people that sent you to kill me," she explained to them. I think her ass is playing good guy and bad guy with her seemingly bipolar ass. She began to stitch the bullet wound closed and the guy was sweating the whole time.

"What's your name?" Vanessa asked the other guy, who ignored her completely. She smiled and stood to her feet before she patted him on the leg and walked away.

"Just tell her man," Bo said to the other guy. If looks could kill, Bo's ass would be dead the way buddy looked at him. In return, Bo shook his head and began to follow Vanessa with his eyes.

She grabbed a really thin knife before she approached the guy again. "What's your name?" she asked calmly. Anytime a female is this calm, something is about to go down.

Vanessa

See the problem with guys these days is they don't take women seriously. For some reason, they don't think women are about that life. I've been growing more and more every day, and I'm learning to respond differently to different situations. Like with the fight with them girls, I wanted to kill them so bad but I knew I could have gone to jail. We were out in the open and anybody could have seen me do what I really wanted to do. Now these niggas, they're free game because they came in here at us. I know nobody in here is going to tell. Well, I know they can't tell without implementing themselves. I almost killed Bo when he spat in my face but I know I needed to keep my cool long enough to find out what I need to know. Plus, I know what I'm going to do to them is going to be enough payback for that spit and then some.

I don't care how many times I had to ask the same question over and over, I'd ask it until I found out who is after who. I have no idea if someone figured out my identity or if someone is after Chris. Either way, I can't rest until I find out what's what.

"What's your name?" I asked the guy Frankie shot. You would think he'd be grateful that I got the bullet out of him before it started to travel. He ignored me completely, like I wasn't being nice. After they came in here to kill us, I'm being as nice as I'm going to be. I stood to my feet and headed to the nightstand, so I could grab my scalpel.

"Just tell her man," Bo said, which caused me to smile slightly. He may not tell me now but he will tell me eventually. Plus, Bo is already so scared of dying that he will tell me anything just to end the pain.

I smiled at the other guy as I got closer to him with my scalpel in hand. "Chris, I need you to pick each finger up for me one at a time," I said, without looking back. I could hear Chris' feet hit the floor when he jumped off the dresser and headed over to me. I waited for him to pick his thumb up as Bo looked at me with his eyes filled with horror. Taking the scalpel, I made small slits between each finger on both hands. "What's your name?" I asked and looked up at the guy.

"That's all you got?" he asked and smiled at me. The smile was replaced with laughter as the room filled with the evilest laugh I've ever heard in my life. "You have no idea who you're dealing with," he said, still laughing. "Even if you kill us, she won't stop. We were just a test of your strength. She won't stop until you're gone," he said as he looked at me in my eyes.

"Who won't stop?" I asked with my heart beating faster and harder by the second.

I could feel myself losing my cool and I was desperately trying to calm down. I needed to know who wanted to kill me and I needed to know why. I'd never done anything to anyone for them to send people to kill me and my friends. I mean, of course my neighbors don't like me because they think I killed their pets, but they had no proof. Yes, I did kill them but nobody saw me do it. I began wracking my brain, trying to figure out who I've wronged and how, but I kept coming up blank. "You'll find out soon enough. If I were you, I wouldn't rush it," he said and snapped me out of my thoughts.

I walked in front of Bo and snatched the salt from its position on the floor. After sprinkling some of it in my hands, I smeared it between each finger, which caused the guy to scream out. I began to breathe heavier and heavier as my cool left. I needed to kill something fast. "Y'all don't have a back door?" I asked Chris. He gave me a confused expression instead of answering, like he was trying to figure out why I needed the back door. I stared at him with a blank expression on my face until he shook his head no. It's fine because I know this apartment is on the outside so the window in Phat's room will lead me outside, and I can simply jog around the building. "I'll be back!" I yelled to Chris before I walked out the room. The guy had finally stopped screaming, so I guess it stopped burning.

I walked in Phat's room and climbed swiftly out the window. I stayed low to the ground and close to the building, as I rounded the back of building. Peeking around the side, the truck was parked in the same spot. With the windows tinted, I couldn't see how many people were in the truck. If they all came together, it wasn't many left. It had to be two left, at the most, and whoever was left had it coming to them. I laid on the ground and rolled over to the next building, so I wouldn't be seen running in between the two buildings. Once I got to the other building, I hopped up and ran low around the building. Even though I was closer to the building, I still couldn't see inside. All I could do at this point was try my luck and hope they hadn't been watching me.

I crept up to the truck and opened the back door as I looked around before I hopped in. Without saying a word, I looked in the area of the truck behind me and no one was there. "What took you so long?" a male voice asked. I turned around and he was in the passenger seat with really dark shades on. I didn't respond, I just stared at him. "Torey," he called out to me.

"Who sent you to kill me?" I asked calmly. I watched as the rise and fall of his chest began to speed up.

"Please, don't kill me. I'm just following orders," he begged me.

"If I don't kill you, she will send you back. I can't take that chance," I said as I watched him lower his head in defeat. I pulled his head back by his hair while slicing his throat at the same time. I sat there and watched as he grabbed his neck, like he was trying to close the cut. The blood continued to pour between his fingers until he took his last breath.

I slid out the backseat of the car and noticed a cab not far away from me with the cabbie sitting in the driver's seat watching me. I could be paranoid but I don't think the cabbies come down here for fares. Last time I checked, you had to walk down to the corner of the street to catch a cab and even then, it was hard because they'd pull off if they thought you were dangerous. I can't just walk back inside the house without seeing what's up with this cabbie. "Fuck it," I said out loud to myself before I walked in the direction of the cab.

As I got closer to it, I could see hair clearly, so I thought it was a woman. It could be the woman that's trying to kill me, so I picked up my pace. I was trying to zoom in on her face but she turned the headlights on and pulled off, headed right at me. She was coming at me full speed when I was jerked out of the way. We both fell to the ground with my body on top of his.

"Why do we keep ending up on the ground?" I asked as I stood to my feet.

"Why the fuck didn't your dumb ass move out the way? You wanted to get hit?" Chris asked me with an attitude.

"Naw, but I wanted to see her face. She turned the headlights on high beam and blinded me though," I responded to his back because he was already walking away from me.

When we entered the apartment, the smell was horrible. "What the fuck is that smell?" I asked because it was not smelling like this before I left out of here.

"Man, you know how they say when someone dies, they release their bowels?" Chris asked as I nodded my head. "Well, it's true," he said and shook his head while headed back into the room. I walked in behind me and the guy I assumed name was Torey was slumped over with foam coming out of his mouth and shit and piss sliding on the floor.

"What the hell happened?" I asked Chris. I glanced at Bo, who was crying silently to himself.

"Man, whatever you put on him had buddy shaking. This nigga started foaming at the mouth and everything until he died and shitted every damn where," Chris explained, all hyped up. "Funniest shit I'd seen in a while," he continued, which caused me to shake my head in disbelief.

"Bo. Who's trying to kill me?" I asked Bo because I was really starting to panic because we were running out of people and were still no closer than we were.

"No, I swear I've never met her," he said as I nodded my response. "You not gone kill me, are you?" he asked, as he was sweating.

"No, I'm not," I answered as Bo sighed deeply, most likely releasing a breath of relief. "He is," I stated and looked over at Chris. He wasted no time pulling out his gun and shooting him.

"You heard that?" I asked Chris.

"Man, the only thing I heard was my gun. What you talking about?" Chris responded to me.

"It sounded like another gun went off at the same time," I said and headed back into the living room. With Chris on my heels, we ran into the living room to find Alexis shot and lying on the floor. I looked over at Frankie and ran to her, only to be caught by Chris.

"Man, you gotta help her. I'm going to carry her in Frankie's room, so you can help her," Chris said to me. I looked over at Phat as he stared at her on the floor.

"I shouldn't have moved. I tried to wake Frankie up and she almost shot me but I jumped out the way," Phat said to me.

I watched Chris scoop Alexis up and carry her to the back room. "VANESSA, COME ON!" Chris yelled and made me run to the back. I just stood there staring at Alexis with tears streaming down my face. All I could think about was losing my only friend and how it was my fault. I shouldn't have given Frankie that medicine or the gun. I knew what would happen if she was woke up with the gun in her hand, but I didn't care. I had tunnel vision and now I was about to lose my only friend right before my eyes. If Alexis died tonight, I promise Frankie will die right after and if I have to kill Chris and Phat too, then so be it.

Whap!

Chris slapped me back into the moment. I ran to my bag and grabbed gloves and peroxide. I placed them on the bed next to Alexis and ran back to get my suture kit. The bullet hit her in the thigh so when Phat moved, he must have hit the gun as well. I know because Frankie is a pretty good shot and the only reason Alexis is still alive is because Phat had to have hit or bumped the gun in some type of way. "Give me a thick belt," I said to Chris and he took off running. He came right back with the belt. "Alexis, I need to tie your hands, so you can't stop me from removing the bullet," I explained as she nodded her head. "I need a small towel," I said to Chris. He opened Frankie's drawer and handed me a shirt. "It's going to hurt so bite down on this," I said to Alexis as she opened her mouth, so I could place the shirt inside. "Chris, come hold her down," I said to Chris, who looked at me crazy. "Man, she won't be able to be still when I start digging!" I snapped him, which caused her eyes to get big.

Chris slowly walked over to us and sat on the bottom half of her legs. After putting gloves on, I started digging. It took about fifteen minutes to get half of the bullet and another twenty to get the other half. Alexis passed out but she was still breathing. I grabbed the peroxide to clean the infection out of the wound. Once it finished, I cleaned it up with alcohol before I stitched it up. I looked through Frankie's drawer for some tights and when I found some I wrapped Alexis' leg tightly to make sure the bleeding stopped. "Let's move her to Phat's room," I said to Chris as I released her arms. He scooped her up, carried her across the hall, and laid her down in the bed. I used two pillows to elevate her leg as I walked back out of the room.

I could see Phat pacing the living room floor as I headed in the direction of the living room. "Is she ok?" he asked as soon as he saw me.

"Yes. She passed out while I was removing the bullet and she hasn't woken up, but she's alive," I said and walked off. I went back into Frankie's room, grabbed a black shirt and some tights, and headed into the bathroom but remembered the dead bodies.

I jogged out to my car to get my machete out of the trunk. It's the one with two blades that I can't keep in my bag because I don't have a case for it and it will cut straight through the bag. Once I got it, I noticed the cab was back. I pretended like I didn't see it as I made my way back into the house.

2 weeks later...
Steve

Things have been going the best they have my whole life since I moved in the Brownstone with Michael. His son Wayne has been by but only once, and he hadn't been able to get a hold of his daughter. I heard him and Wayne talking about her but not into detail. It was more so of father and brother being worried about her. I also heard Wayne telling his dad he didn't think I should be staying here, since they know little to nothing about me. I don't blame him though because there was nothing on file for me when I was locked up. He hadn't brought that up though, but I saw the black residue on my fingers, so I know they tried fingerprinting me.

It was kind of odd being here because whenever Michael called his daughter, he would walk away to leave a message. Wayne was telling him something bad that she's been doing but when they noticed me within ear shot, they stopped talking. I've never had an actual family but I guess they keep each other's secrets. The thing about that is, Michael's a homicide detective protecting his daughter. I bet she could get away with anything she's doing because I'm sure he's going to cover up her tracks.

"I'm going out," Michael said and snapped me back into now. Every day before he goes to work, he left out, probably looking for his daughter. I looked through his notes and saw several addresses, something about bus 91, a name Princess, and cab 4141. I had no idea what any of it meant. These are personal notes though, so Princess must be his daughter.

"Alright," I said anxious for him to leave, so I could go back into his office. There has to be more information in there, so I could help him find his daughter. I know people that will talk to me but won't talk to him because he's a cop.

When he left out of the door, I waited ten minutes before I went back into his room. I looked all over the place and couldn't find anything! I began searching through his drawers when I heard a gun cock. Turning around slowly, I was face to face with Michael. "What are you looking for?" he asked with the gun trained on my head. I didn't respond right away because

I was trying to figure out how he got back in without me hearing him. I know I wasn't that deep into finding what I was looking for not to hear him.

"It's not what you think. I was only trying to help," I said with my arms in the air. Shit, had I known he wasn't gone or was trying to catch me, I wouldn't have come back in here trying to look.

"Help me do what, exactly?" he asked without removing the gun from in front of my face.

"Find your daughter, Princess," I said as I watched his facial expression soften.

"Man, I thought you were trying to rob me after I let you live here for free," he said and made me understand why he had a gun on me in the first place.

"We can go in the morning to look for her together," he said as he gestured for me to get out of his room. I nodded my head while walking out of the room. He closed the door and I could hear light sobs coming from inside his room. He must really miss his daughter. I can't believe she ran away from a good home like this. From the looks of those addresses, she must be living from pillow to post.

I can't do anything but shake my head at her and hope she comes home soon because a dad needs their daughter, just as much as a daughter need their dad. I would never leave a home like this on my own, which is why I hadn't left here since I got here, not even to go to the store. I hadn't left at all! I'm not sure if my apartment is still up or if Chris and Phat had been looking for me or nothing because quite frankly, I just don't care.

Phat

I hadn't let Alexis out of my sight since she got shot by Frankie. Frankie's ass been apologizing every other day too. She acts like we don't know she disappears whenever Vanessa comes home because she doesn't know what she's going to do to her. I think Vanessa was over it that night though. Vanessa struck me as the type of person that if she's going to do something to you, it's gonna happen sooner rather than later. Plus, she's been so busy with all these hits back to back, she's barely even been home to see her folks.

Alexis kept telling her that her dad had been looking for her, but she would always say she would call him as soon as she caught a break and was able to sit down long enough to talk to him. I could tell she was tired but she just kept going. Chris had been telling me every time he left our new place, it would be a cab sitting outside. He told me he tried to get in twice and both times she would pull off before he got close enough to her to see her face. It has to be the same cabbie that did me like that the night Alexis got shot. I hadn't mentioned anything to Vanessa or Alexis about it because I wanted to check it out myself first.

"Where you going babe?" Alexis asked me as I was headed out of the door.

"I'm about to stand outside," I answered as I headed out the room. We had a four bedroom two-bathroom brownstone now. That night all that shit happened, we knew we couldn't stay there anymore. Not with the stench of death and blood, plus we had no idea where Steve had been hiding. I didn't know the nigga was that resourceful to disappear off the face of the earth. I just hope he hadn't gotten himself killed because I want to kill him.

I stepped out on the porch just as the cab was pulling up. I walked on the sidewalk on the opposite side of the road with my head down, like I hadn't noticed her. With my head down, I could glance at her without spooking her. I could see her long flowing jet black hair clearly. I stopped right next to the cab and looked directly at her as she looked back at me. We were just staring at each other for several seconds as I thought about how unprepared I am right now. I don't have a gun or anything right now.

"Babe!" Alexis yelled, which caused me to look in her direction.

"What are you doing?" she asked as she looked from me to the cab. The last thing I want her to do was think I'm cheating on her. I looked back at the cabbie who was looking at Alexis like she knew her. As soon as I took a step closer, she pulled off and looked completely down when she got near Alexis.

"Did you see her face?" I asked Alexis as I jogged up to her.

"What? No. What's going on?" she asked me.

"Fuck!" I said as I stormed passed her to call Chris. When I found my phone, he answered on the third ring.

"What's good?" Chris asked.

"Man, find Nessa and come here so we can talk. It's time to discuss this cabbie for real," I said to Chris over the phone.

"Iight bet," Chris said and hung up.

Chris showed up about thirty minutes later and it took Vanessa another hour or so after that. I wonder what the hell she be doing, especially since the cabbie is possibly looking for her.

Vanessa

I'd had fifteen hits in two weeks, so I'd been extremely exhausted. Especially since when I'm not working, I'm looking for Steve. I have no earthly idea where he could be. Both Phat and Steve said he didn't have anyone other than them, so I figured he'd come up for air eventually but it hasn't happened. On top of that, I'd fallen in love with Chris. He's so not how I thought he was. I guess every guy will change but it has to be for the one they actually want to be with. I know people can be with someone for years just because it's convenient and not really love them. I think both parties will end up hurting if one isn't all the way in and that's what I'm afraid of. Well, it isn't like I'd had experience being with someone because guys normally don't pay me any attention. They normally go for the girls with the big booty and big breast, and let's just say I'm the complete opposite.

The night those guys forced their way in on us and he kissed me, I could have melted right there in his arms but I needed to get down to business. We needed to find out who sent them and why. All I was able to find out was a woman sent them to kill me. We set the apartment on fire and left. Well, I set it on fire because everyone else was against it. I knew the fire would burn all traces of evidence and we wouldn't be implicated in the crime. They only objected because of the fact that other people lived there but I knew someone would call the police. I had been watching the news and the only dead bodies found were the ones we left.

I took about $50,000 and got us a Brownstone. The payments from the hits allowed me to furnish the house completely and buy everyone a new wardrobe. I still had about $90,000 left and people were still calling me to set up hits. The plan is to take a week off to rest and have dinner with my dad, who had been calling me every day for a while now. Well, every day since everything has gone down. I told him I had my own place and he could come by whenever he wanted to, but he hadn't made an appearance yet. Not that I was ever there. With the way the hits been happening, I'd only been there to sleep.

Ring, Ring

"Hey daddy" I answered the phone.

"What have you been doing that's keeping you too busy to come see your old man?" he asked, getting straight to the point.

"Just working. I been really busy working. Sorry. I was about to take next week off to spend some time with you," I said to him feeling bad. I really miss my dad but work isn't the only reason I stay away from him. He has a way of reading people and I can't have him figuring out what I do for a living.

"Ok Princess," he said, which caused me to pull the phone away from my ear and look at it. I didn't respond right away because I didn't know if he was calling me his Princess or if he knew what I had been doing. "See you tomorrow morning at the point. Be there at 9am. I have some things to handle and discuss with you and your friends. Plus, I have a surprise for you," he continued and shocked me completely.

"Yes sir. I love you, daddy," I said to him.

"I love you too," he said before he disconnected the call.

After hanging up with him, I looked up and saw my latest target walking out the bank. He hopped in his off white Porsche and pulled out into traffic with me following as close behind him as possible. "Yea," I answered my phone without looking at it.

"Aye, Phat said come home so he can tell us some stuff," Chris said into my ear.

"Alright, be there shortly," I responded and disconnected the call. I couldn't afford to get distracted by thoughts of Chris and miss my target.

See, I'd been watching him a few days and he's only alone when he goes to the bank. If I can't stop him before he gets home, I'll miss him again. I decide to cut him off and play the damsel in distress. I discovered a shortcut that will get me closer to his house faster than him. I'm not worried about how fast he drives because he purposely takes the long way home.

I pulled over about ten miles away from his house, parked on the side of the road, and popped the hood before stepping out. I had on some cut-off jean shorts and a t shirt, so I cut the bottom half of it off to show more skin. Looking in the trunk, I slid on my custom made stiletto heels with the bottom hollowed out. The heels of the shoes were the sharpest Japanese blades known to man. Inside the shoe was a paralyzing agent released upon blade to skin contact. I got these shoes made specifically for this multi-millionaire HIV infected broker. According to the letter, he had been going around purposely infecting women with the virus simply because he had it. Unfortunately for them to not only get it but to either not know they had it or not be able to afford the medication to treat it. Safe sex is the best sex. Don't risk your life just because it feels better when it's unprotected. I almost took this job for free just because of the principle of it but a girl still has to eat.

It took about twenty minutes for him to come around the corner and I was bent over the hood as he passed right by me. "Fuck!" I said out loud to myself as I took a squat with my head down and tried to figure out another way to get him.

"You need some help miss?" I heard a smooth voice say behind me. When I turned around, I saw my target standing directly in front of me. He was tall and muscular, mocha colored skin with a taper fade and waves that will make you sea sick. He smiled a perfect smile with perfect white teeth and everything about him screamed money! Luckily for me, I already know this charming handsome guy is the grim reaper.

"I think my car ran hot," I said as I slowly turned around to look at the engine, like I knew what I was looking at.

"Let me take a look," he said as he took a step closer to me and removed his suit jacket and button up shirt. His muscles were so defined and he was a walking work of art with all of the tattoos that draped his arms, chest and back.

I stood next to him as he examined a car that nothing is wrong with. "Damn girl, I think your radiator hose has a hole in it. You need me to give you a lift anywhere?" he asked as he licked his lips seductively and stared me directly in my eyes. Instead of responding, I closed the hood of my car, hopped on top of it, and laid flat against it before I pulled one leg to me. He smiled, unbuttoned his slacks, and took a step closer to me, then freed the biggest dick I'd ever seen! He grabbed my leg and held it up in the air before pulling his muscle shirt off. He rubbed his muscular hand down my leg, which caused me to moan out in pleasure. He let go of my leg and I wrapped them both around his waist, allowing one of my heels to lightly penetrate the skin of his back.

"You like fucking on hoods out in the open?" he asked as he stared directly in my eyes.

"I'd rather you fuck me hard on top of your car," I said and pointed at his Porsche. He stood up straight before he began to sway. "Are you ok?" I asked him as his legs gave and caused him to hit the ground. "Oh my gosh! Sir! What do I do?" I asked as I pretended I didn't know what was happening.

When I was sure he wouldn't be able to hurt me, I sat on my knees right next to him. "You were gonna give me a death sentence just like you've been giving everyone else huh?" I asked, which caused his eyes to widen in disbelief. "Now, I'm giving you a faster one. Not only did I inject you with a paralyzing agent, but I'm going to sit here and watch you die. See, first you won't be able to move like now, next each organ will shut down one by one and do you want to know the real kicker?" I asked as I watched a tear fall down the side of his head.

"I'm sorry. Please don't," he said, as if I could stop what was happening.

"You're going to feel every bit of it," I said as I stood to my feet. I watched him die and more than likely it happened so fast because the pain stopped his heart.

I threw my shoes back in the trunk and headed home.

Chris

I was out getting into something when Phat called me and told me to find Vanessa and come home, so we could talk. I called her to tell her and we disconnected the call.

"Why you always answer the phone like you ain't with me?" Brittany asked.

"Because man, I don't know what's going on or what done happened," I answered her, which caused her to roll her eyes at me. I could tell she had an attitude and with a female like this, I know exactly how to fix it. I started to slowly move in and out of her before I picked up the pace. I know you thinking, 'no this nigga didn't answer the phone while he was fucking', but I did. I went from giving her long slow strokes to long, fast, and hard strokes. She was nutting in a matter of minutes!

"Fuck! Chris! Mmmmhhh!" she moaned out. I needed to make this nut quick, so I could get to the house and see what was going on.

"You about to go?" Brittany asked while she watched me get dressed.

"Yea. I'll hit you later," I said and walked towards the door. I didn't miss the sad look she gave me; I just didn't give a fuck. Brittany got some good pussy and amazing head, and that's the only reason I talk to her at all. Crazy thing about that is she knew it. A nigga will only do what you allow him to do. Females be complaining about what their significant other did to them, but what y'all don't realize is everything he's doing now, he will continue to do because he got away with it. With Brittany, I hope like hell she doesn't think that its anything more with us than sex, especially since she been fucking me and Phat for years now.

When I pulled up to our new place, I parked my car. Yes, I said *my car*. Vanessa's ass didn't want any of us bringing heat to her business and she felt like us stealing cars and robbing niggas would bring heat to her, so she bought us all cars. Her little is ass so generous, it's crazy. I love her to death already but we not in a relationship or even working on one. She's still holding on to that fight we got in, not realizing that it wouldn't have happened if she would have either told me why she didn't want to eat in the kitchen or just didn't eat in my room. She's stuck on the fact that I'd hit her, so she thinks I'd hit her again. She isn't dating anyone though, so it's not like I have to see her be with someone else.

I walked in the house and Phat, Alexis, and Frankie were all sitting in the living room waiting on us. "Where's Vanessa?" Alexis asked.

"We don't be gone together. She ain't fucking with ya boy," I said and walked out of the living room.

"What you fina do?" Phat asked me.

"Wash my nuts," I said as I walked in my room to get my clothes. I took a quick shower and when I got out, Vanessa still wasn't there.

"Call her back," Alexis said to me like they aren't the ones that are best friends.

"Man, you call her," I said and sat down. The door opened a few seconds later and in walked Vanessa with some little ass shorts on and a ripped t-shirt, which caused my blood to boil instantly!

"The fuck you got on?!" I snapped at her.

She laughed to herself before she shook her head and took a seat on the La-Z-Boy chair. "What's up?" she asked Phat and completely ignored me.

"So listen," Phat began.

"No, fuck that! Go put some damn clothes on!" I yelled and stood up.

"Chris, chill," Phat said to me.

"Naw, you wouldn't let Alexis wear that shit either!" I snapped at Phat.

"Difference is Alexis is his girlfriend. I'm single," Vanessa said and pissed me off. I stood up, snatched her out of the chair, and pulled her back to her room.

I pushed her in her room, slammed the door behind us, and locked it. "Change clothes," I stated calmly.

"For fucking what? Who's it killing?" she asked with her hands on her hips.

I didn't respond to her. I just went to her dresser and pulled out a t-shirt and sweat pants. "Put this on," I said as I tossed the clothes at her.

"No," she said and tossed them on her bed. I walked up to her so fast, she thought I was about to hit her. I know because I grabbed her by her shoulders and stopped her from dropping low to spin kick me. I think that's her favorite fucking move but I'd learned to time her perfectly, so she better come up with a new move.

"Why won't you change clothes?" I asked her as I pulled her up into my arms.

"Why do it matter?" she asked as she squirmed and tried to get free. I let her arms go, grabbed her face, and kissed her lips. She resisted at first but gave in when her body went limp in my arms. "Change clothes," I said once I pulled away from her.

I stood there and watched as she pulled her shirt off followed by her shorts, like I wasn't standing there. I could feel my man rising to the occasion, like I hadn't just relieved him of all pressure. She slipped into the jogging pants and t-shirt and left out of the room. I had to give it a few minutes and adjustment before I followed her out.

Vanessa

"I don't know why you won't just give him a try," Alexis said to me as soon as I walked into the living room fully dressed.

"Because he's still fucking Brittany," I replied nonchalantly. I never told Chris that's the reason when he asked me because its more than that. Chris hit me and I don't think a man should ever hit a woman. If it comes to us fighting, he should be man enough to walk away. Secondly, he's controlling and I'm not well behaved. It may start with him telling me what I can and can't wear but eventually, it will be where I can and can't go. Then on top of that, he's still fucking Brittany and Tiffany, while trying to get with me. If I get with him while he's still messing with them, he will continue to mess with them. Not to mention I know he's still having sex with them because they're good at whatever it is they're doing to him. Since I'm a virgin, I'm sure I'm not good at anything and I don't want to set myself up for heartbreak.

I sat down in the living room followed by Chris a few minutes later. "So, check this out," Phat said as he stood up. "I don't know if y'all been paying attention or not but since that night, a lady in a cab been following us. I noticed when I first left y'all to go get Alexis. She was parked where the cabs were but when I tried to get in, she pulled off. A black Tahoe truck almost ran me over and when I looked up, she was watching me before pulling off," Phat said, which made me think back to that night as well. Sadly, I hadn't paid much attention to cabs and she could have been following me too.

"Wait a minute. When I was leaving the house that night, I saw her too but I didn't try to get in her cab," Alexis said. "Was it the same lady from earlier?" Alexis asked Phat.

"Earlier?" I asked as Phat nodded his head.

"That's why I wanted to talk to y'all. I don't know what she want or who she want," Phat said to me.

"That night all that shit went down, after I killed the blind guy, I saw a cab. I was about to walk up to it but she was about to run me over," I said.

"Yeah and I pulled her dumb ass out the way," Chris said as he shook his head.

"I talked to my daddy. He called me Princess and told me to meet him tomorrow morning and to bring y'all," I told the group. Everyone nodded their head except Chris. "What's wrong?" I asked and looked at Chris.

"Yo daddy a fuckin cop! How we know this ain't a set up?" he asked, which pissed me off.

"Because he's my damn daddy. And because he knows where we live, so he could have sent the folks here," I said as I shook my head at him.

We talked and chilled a few more minutes before everyone went to their rooms. I hopped in the shower and laid across my bed as I turned Netflix on. I wanted to catch up on The Walking Dead from season 1, so I would understand what was going on.

Knock, Knock

"It's unlocked," I said to Chris. I already knew it was him because Alexis doesn't knock, Frankie pretty much stays away from me, and Phat doesn't come in my room at all. Chris walked in wearing only basketball shorts and tube socks as he crawled in my bed. He does this from time to time but I'm not sure why. He will randomly come in here and lay with me while watching TV, and then go in his room and go to sleep.

"What we watching?" he asked after he got comfortable.

"The Walking Dead," I answered him.

"You always watching weird shit," he said.

"And you're always watching with me."

"Touché," he replied simply.

We watched two seasons of The Walking Dead before we fell asleep together. It was the first time we ever stayed a full night and morning together.

Phat

Heading to meet Vanessa's dad was kind of awkward, considering our line of work and his. Him being a homicide detective and his daughter being a murderer. If he called her by her work name, that means he knows what she does. If he wanted us to come with her, then he also knows what we do. I can understand Chris' hesitancy but at the same time, I know he's going to protect his daughter by any means.

We decided to take the Expedition Vanessa bought for trips she wanted us to start taking. Vanessa's one of those people that if she loves you, there's nothing she won't do for you. If she got it, you got it and she's growing on me more and more each day. I really thought she was crazy when Alexis use to tell me about her. Well shit, I still think she's crazy but I understand her crazy now, and I love her because Alexis loves her.

We all hopped out the truck at the same time and walked into the building without a care in the world. Her dad was sitting in a chair waiting on us when we walked in. "Hey daddy," Vanessa said and walked up to him giving him a hug.

"Hey sweetheart," he said as he kissed her on the forehead.

"How have you been?" she asked him.

"Missing you. Come on, I have a surprise for you," he said and pulled her behind him. "Y'all too, c'mon!" he yelled over his shoulder.

Vanessa

I didn't realize how much I missed my daddy until I saw him when we walked in the building. I was still confused about why I needed to bring everyone for us to talk about me. We followed him down the hall until we got right outside of a door with a small slot at eye level. "Listen sweetheart, I know what you do for a living but you have to be more careful. I've been putting everything together because you leave small pieces of yourself. Now if I wasn't your dad, I wouldn't have been able to figure out that you were the culprit," my dad said to me as I nodded my head. I didn't need to respond because he's right.

"As for y'all, I know y'all stopped what y'all were doing but you need to get jobs or something. Vanessa is bringing in too much money for her to be the only one working in that big nice brownstone y'all got over there," he said as he looked back at them. "Chris?" he asked with his hand out stretched towards him.

"Yes sir," Chris said, who shocked me with the pleasantries and shook my dad's hand.

"Take care of my daughter. I can tell you love her but you have to let that other stuff go before she will give you a chance," he said then turned back to me. I was shocked because I didn't know he knew me as well as he does.

"I'm going to open this door and you guys have to be cool while I tell you what happened and what has been going on," he said to us, which caused me to become anxious. He turned his back to us as he unlocked the door. I glanced back at Chris, who winked at me before focusing his attention back on the door. When he let us in, I could see a body on the table with a sheet over it confusing me.

I followed closely behind him to the table as he snatched the sheet off the body. "Steve?" Phat asked as he stepped closer. Steve's eyes got big as he looked into the faces of people he once called his brothers and sister. I looked at Frankie and she had tears streaming down her cheeks. I swear I'd think she was pregnant if she ever left the house or brought someone over because she's so emotional. Alexis had her head down and shook it, while Phat and Chris both stared at Steve tied to the table by the restraints they use at the hospital to hold people down.

"So, I've found out a few things you guys probably want to know that Steve may or may not disclose," my dad said as he talked to Phat and Chris.

"Why man?" Phat asked as he stared at Steve, who just looked away.

"I'm thinking jealousy for some reason," my dad said and took Phat's and Chris' attention away from Steve. "You guys robbed a few houses over in Newark. Steve told them it was James and his crew. They caught up to James and told him to bring you guys to them. I don't know why you all didn't show up or what happened, but it was all a set up," my dad explained, which caused them to shake their heads. They knew it was a setup, just didn't know that it all happened because of Steve. "Vanessa, the guy's brother they robbed is the guy that hired you to kill the guys that were about to kill them. He had no idea that you were going to show up the same night as the setup. He was trying to kill two birds with one stone. Allowing his brother to kill them and for you to kill his brother would have put him on top. After his plan backfired, he linked up with the lady that drives cab 4141. I've tried to get close enough to her to see her face but every time I try, she pulls off. I normally only see her watching one of you guys," my dad said to me.

Standing here listening to everything my dad was telling me had me zoning out. It was a lot to take in at once and kind of had me rethinking my line of work. Nobody knows who this lady is or why she wants to kill me. I don't even know who hired me but since my dad knows, we can find him and get him to tell us who she is. "Any questions?" my dad asked.

"We need to find the guy that hired me that night, so we can figure out who this woman is," I said as everyone nodded their heads in agreement.

"Ok, do what you want with him," my dad said and stepped to the side.

"You brought your bag Nessa?" Chris asked me.

"Of course. It's in the truck. I'll run out and get it," I said as I headed towards the door.

BOOM

Somebody threw a flash grenade in the room and blinded me instantly. I couldn't see or hear anything as I tried to make my way out of the room. I was dizzy and eventually fell over onto my back. The room filled with smoke and I could see people running passed me. My vision slowly started coming back and I could see the table Steve was on being rolled passed me out the door. I couldn't see my dad, Alexis, Phat, or Chris, so I don't know if they were okay or not. I could hear high heeled shoes headed in my direction.

"You want me to kill her boss?" I heard a male voice say.

"Not yet. It's too easy this way," a woman replied. I laid there in a daze as I watched her silhouette get closer to me until she was squatting next to me. I could see her face as clear as day. My heart beat sped up and my breath got caught in my throat.

"Mom?" was the last thing I said before everything went black.

TRUE GLORY PUBLICATIONS

IF YOU WOULD LIKE TO BE A PART OF OUR TEAM, PLEASE SEND YOUR SUBMISSIONS BY EMAIL TO TRUEGLORYPUBLICATIONS@GMAIL.COM. PLEASE INCLUDE A BRIEF BIO, A SYNOPSIS OF THE BOOK, AND THE FIRST THREE CHAPTERS. SUBMIT USING MICROSOFT WORD WITH FONT IN 11 TIMES NEW ROMAN.

Check Out These Other Great Books from This Author

Addicted To Him

Please Read These Other Great Books from True Glory
Publications

Certified Bosset 4

The Daughter Of Black Ice

No Respect For A weak Man 2